P9-DXF-754

MARY

UNLEASHED

MARY

UNLEASHED

HILLARY MONAHAN

HYPERION

LOS ANGELES | NEW YORK

First edition, September 2015
1 3 5 7 9 10 8 6 4 2
G475-5664-5-15166
Printed in the United States of America

Library of Congress Cataloging-in-Publication for Hardcover
Monahan, Hillary.
    Mary : unleashed/Hillary Monahan.—First Hyperion Hardcover edition.
        pages cm.— (Bloody Mary ; Book 2)
    Summary: Jess McAllister's summoning obsession has turned into a
deadly haunting since the ghost of Mary Worth will not rest until Jess has
come undone, so now it is up to Jess and her reluctant friends, Shauna and
Kitty, to stop Mary for good.
    ISBN 978-1-4231-8539-0 (hardback)
[1. Horror stories.   2. Ghosts—Fiction.   3. Supernatural—Fiction.
4. Friendship—Fiction.]   I. Title.
    PZ7.M73655Mat 2015
    [Fic]—dc23   2014047136

Visit www.hyperionteens.com

For Lauren, who's been there through every step of this journey

June 24, 1864

Sister Mine,

Below, I have listed my dastardly deeds since you abandoned me for Boston. "But Mary," you say. "I did not abandon you so much as find a handsome gentleman to kiss me breathless for eternity." The result is the same, Constance. I have brought a reign of terror to Solomon's Folly. I will not be sated until I have tainted everything you love with my terribleness.

1. I have claimed your room as my own. The pink sashes are gone because pink is an affront to all that is good in the world. I have replaced it with a shade of green you would abhor. I do this as both a declaration of war and because green is a far superior color.

2. I have taken over your gardening duties. This is not to help Mother but to destroy your handiwork. Plants wither in fear at the sight of my boots. I am not blessed with your green thumb but, as Mother says, a black thumb, and I shall use it to wreak havoc upon your peonies.

3. I have taken your place on the church choir. The psalms you hold so dear are now sung so off pitch, dogs bay thinking me their pack mistress. Our sweet mother has asked if perhaps I would like to do a Sunday reading in lieu of the hymnals, but I remain stalwart.

(To her chagrin, I might add. When I expressed that I preferred the music, she looked much like your peonies—wilted and sad.)

4. Despite your instruction that the shawl you knitted me last winter should not be worn with my shapeless blue frock, I have done just that. I disavow fashion! I want those who look upon me to know repulsion and fear. Your innocent lace is a weapon in my hands.

5. I have taken over your duties with the Spencer girls, and I believe they find me the superior nanny. What better way to vex you than to fatten up the children you love with so much shortbread, they explode. Whilst Mrs. Spencer will undoubtedly take offense to my practices, the children will love me best, and that is all that matters.

   (I caught Agatha with two meaty fists in the shortbread pan. The child had eaten half the contents in the three minutes I took to attend her sister's nappies. I would have been impressed if I was not so horribly afraid she'd get sick.)

6. Mr. Biscuits is a traitor. Your poorly named dog has all but forgotten you. He sleeps at the foot of my bed every night making terrible sounds and equally as terrible smells. Every morning he looks upon me like I am the sun in his furry little world. This is likely because I am the one to feed him the scraps, but let's pretend he is drawn to my shining disposition.

7. Not only did I not go to the summer dance, I told Thomas Adderly that I would rather wash my hair than attend. I did not do this simply because Thomas is overly ardent and annoying. No, it was to defy your terrible sisterly advice! For shame, Constance! For shame!

(Honestly, the boy is dull, and I've seen better teeth in horse mouths. There's also the Elizabeth Hawthorne problem. Her preference for dull, horse-teethed gentlemen causes me far too much grief. While attending a dance may have been nice, the company was lacking and the repercussions weren't worthwhile.)

8. Last, but by no means least, I cancel my trek to Boston. Fie upon you and your fancy home! I shall remain in Solomon's Folly until my skin is withered and my teeth fall out!

   (I am suffering a summer cold that has wetted my lungs, and Mother says I must wait to travel. While I do not like postponing, my sickness has kept me abed the last few days. I will write you when I am less apt to play the part of Pestilence. I hope to reschedule soon.)

I hope this letter finds you miserable (blissfully happy) and that Joseph snores in his sleep. (That would be awful. Mr. Biscuits is bad enough. A full-grown man must be thrice as disruptive.)

Write soon, my beloved harpy.

Your sister,

Mary

1

The darkness has a face.

Gray skin stretched over a craggy skull, black veins pulsing at the temples and cheeks. It has no nose, no lips—only voids crusted with liquid decay. Broken teeth jut up from the gums like yellow stalagmites. A white, wormlike tongue wags to taste the air. Tufts of hair top half-rotted ears, leaves and debris tangled in the elbow-length strands.

The darkness has a voice. Sometimes it's wet, like pipes choking through a clog. Other times it's dry and slithery, like snake scales gliding over rock. It depends on whether she's laughing. Mary likes to laugh, but only if she's bled someone. That's when the raspiest rattles echo from her throat.

Nothing is normal after a haunting. School, friends, boys . . . who cares? How can you worry about the mundane when you've seen the extraordinary? When one of your best friends was killed by a ghost before your eyes?

I still can't look in a mirror, because I see her. Mary. She's tattooed on my brain. Vines swathing her thin frame, clinging to a ragged dress with a copper-splattered bodice. Talons tipping the spindly fingers, the edges as sharp as razors. One leg swollen with water and ready to burst, the other nothing but bone. Beetles everywhere, living inside a walking corpse, scurrying beneath the skin until they gnaw their way out.

The thought of her is enough to send me fleeing to my mother's side. Last week, I caught a glimpse of my reflection in a picture frame and hit the floor as if I were in an air raid. Mom doesn't understand my twitchiness. Worse, I can't explain it. She would never believe me. I hadn't believed Jess when she'd first told me about it, either.

Jess. She got us into this mess. Bloody Mary Worth was her obsession and we were stupid enough to follow. When Jess positioned us in that bathroom, when she checked her compass points and placed the candle and salt line, we didn't think anything would happen. It was just a game. Then a ghostly hand pressed against the glass. We should have ended it there, but one more summon, Jess said. Just one. I relented. No, I encouraged my friends to go along with it because I was curious.

Now I'm scarred, Jess is haunted, and Anna's dead. Regret weighs on me from the moment I wake in the morning until I drift into my dreams. I want to walk away, to let Mary be Jess's problem, but I have a debt to repay. To Anna. To other girls who'd play the game. Jess will pawn the ghost onto someone sooner or later. Mary will continue torturing girls from the mirror.

I have to do something about it.
The question is . . . what?

∽

The letter from Mary to Constance Worth Simpson should have made me laugh. It should have warmed me to the authoress from a century and a half ago. I'd have thought her clever and charming. I'd have said something like, "I'd be her friend."

But this letter had been stuffed inside of Jess McAllister's notebook, wedged between two pages of handwritten notes about Bloody Mary. Despite the tone, it was no joke, as proven by the three other letters present. They cataloged Mary's plight from start to end—a smart, funny teenager deteriorating along with her circumstances. A cruel pastor robbing her of her mother, and in turn her humor. Anger filled the gaps, but eventually that was taken, too, when she was murdered at seventeen years old.

The ghost of the legend wasn't born evil. She was made that way. Two cups tragedy, one tablespoon cruelty, a splash of neglect. It was a recipe for pain.

We tried to stop Mary. Jess even staged another summoning with Kitty, Laurie Carmichael, and Becca Miller, "To save you, Shauna," she said to me. "To get you unhaunted." She succeeded, albeit not how she anticipated. Jess planned for Kitty to take on the curse during that last summoning, but I intervened and Jess was grabbed in Kitty's stead.

We sent Mary back into the mirror, but not before Mary spilled Jess's blood. We all knew what that meant; Mary wouldn't let Jess go until Jess died or another girl took the mark from her. It was how it had always been with Bloody Mary. It was how it would be until someone put the ghost to rest. More girls would die.

Like Anna Sasaki died.

It was hard to believe she was gone. Some days, the pain of her loss was raw, like someone branding me with a hot poker. Other days, it was a dull throb, like a bone-deep bruise. I missed Anna's intelligence. I missed her snark. I missed scribbling notes to her during math class to pass the time.

I missed *her*.

School resumed a few days after her disappearance. AMBER Alert: Anna Sasaki. The police hadn't a trace, nor would they find one: Mary dragged Anna through the mirror and into her swampy, black world.

The fog rising on the other side of the mirror. Crimson blood spraying across the glass. Too much to be nonfatal. Too much to grant any hope that Anna survived. Terror and loss and futility dropping on my head like an anvil. Grief crushing me beneath its weight.

The Sasakis would never get the closure they so deserved.

The days after the murder were a fixed reel in a movie, the same twelve-hour clip playing, rewinding, and repeating the next morning. I got up, ate breakfast with my mother, and went to school early. I didn't like being alone in the house. Every sound in the building sent me scurrying for the only weapon I knew that worked against Mary—salt. It burned her. I had boxes of it squirreled away in my closet in case she returned.

There was no reason to expect her, but Jess's tie to Mary made me uneasy. Would Jess's haunting be different because she and Mary were related? What would happen if Jess somehow allied with Mary? I put nothing past Jess. She'd sacrificed one friend to the mirror and nearly succeeded in sacrificing a second.

Jess could justify anything when she put her mind to it. Even murder.

At the end of the school day, I would go to Kitty's house until Mom got out of work. After Anna died, Mom cut her hours at her second job. It was the only good thing to come from the haunting. I loved my mom. I also loved knowing that Mary left me alone whenever Mom was near. We never quite figured out why that was, but I had my suspicions. Mary Worth loved her mother. Other mothers were safe by association.

I spent the last hour of every day alone in my room, lying in bed and gazing at the wall. My thoughts drifted to Anna, to Kitty's boyfriend, Bronx. He was a star football player before Mary pulled him through a glass window and dropped him three stories. His legs had snapped like twigs. Double casts, metal bolts, surgeries—he was lucky he'd ever walk again, never mind play sports.

Mary took so much from both of them. Thinking about my part in bringing her into this world almost always made me weep into my pillow. It would have been easy to lay it all on Jess, but I wouldn't fool myself. I'd made bad decisions, too.

Jess liked to remind me of that sometimes. She refused to fade into obscurity. Rapid-fire texts—sometimes apologies, sometimes accusations. I ignored every message. The assault died down after the first few weeks, but I'd still get the occasional plea for help. When she saw me in the halls at school—her eyes sunken in like she hadn't slept in forever, a fresh cut or scratch marring her skin—I looked away. Sometimes she followed me, calling my name. I ducked into classrooms to avoid her. I left the cafeteria if she tried to eat near me.

It wasn't just because of what she did. The cuts and bruises told me she hadn't lost Mary yet. No one near Jess McAllister was safe.

∽

"Shauna, wait up!"

Kitty's voice sliced through the hall din. The last bell had rung, and kids were eager to exit the school. We were only a week away from summer vacation, and you could feel the anticipation in the air. The chatter was louder and more animated. The attitudes in class were more laissez-faire. I resented it. Anna's death plagued me every day, while my classmates talked about beach parties. It was too soon. I wasn't ready for life to go on.

Kitty trotted up to my locker, her book bag slung over her shoulder. Her face was flushed from gym, her heavyset body hugged by a tank top and shorts. She hadn't changed clothes from class, but then, neither of us could go into the girls' locker room. That's where Anna went missing. Kitty usually opted to change in her car. I snuck off to change in the bathrooms near the science labs, my trusty box of salt perched on the toilet tank.

Kitty swept a lock of caramel-brown hair away from her ear.

"Let's get out of here. Tennis in ninety-degree heat is not fun. I'll roll the windows down in case I stink. Sorry."

"No problem." We shouldered our way through the hallway and out the back doors. My backpack weighed fifteen thousand pounds. Finals were upon us, and though I tried to study for the tests, I couldn't focus. It was like all my textbooks had spontaneously rewritten themselves in a language I didn't understand.

"I'm avoiding the principal's office now," Kitty said as we approached her red SUV. "There's a memorial for Anna in one of the display cases. Every time I see it, I cry."

Saying Anna's name was enough to make Kitty's voice hitch. I squeezed her shoulder, doing my best to ignore the sweat slicking her skin. Kitty and Anna had been best friends since grade school. Losing Anna on top of Bronx's accident—if you can call it an accident when a ghost flings your boyfriend out a window—had ruined her. Looking at Anna's picture every day would be a special kind of torture.

"I'm sorry. At least we're almost done with school. You'll get a few months off to recoup."

Kitty tossed her stuff into the back of the car before climbing into the driver's side. "Not exactly. We're still doing that thing with Cody in Solomon's Folly."

I wasn't the only one feeling obligated to end Mary Worth. I told Kitty time and time again that I could handle it without her, that Cody Jackson had volunteered to help so Kitty could stay safe, but Kitty always threw my own words back at me: we'd walked away with our lives, but others might not be so lucky.

We had to do something.

"We started it together, we'll finish it together. For Anna," she'd say.

It was always we. It was always for Anna.

I couldn't quite look at Kitty's profile. If I'd told Jess no all those weeks ago, if I'd been less of a pushover...

"It's okay, Shauna."

She brushed the back of my hand, her fingers tan next to my pasty, befreckled skin. It wasn't absolution, but it was enough. Kitty put the key in the ignition, opening the windows and sunroof of the truck. A breeze swept in, pushing the oppressive heat away.

As soon as Kitty inched from the parking spot, a green Ford Focus sailed around the line of cars and stopped in front of us. Kitty slammed on the brakes. My hand gripped the dash as I peered down the expanse of the SUV's hood only to find myself staring at Jess McAllister. So blond. So perfect with that narrow nose and big blue eyes. So *injured*. A ragged cut bisected her right cheek and top lip. I'd passed her in the hall just yesterday and the cut hadn't been there.

How'd she explain that to her family? A fight? A bear encounter? She tripped and fell on a shovel?

My pulse pounded in my ears.

She shouted something that the end-of-school-day chaos drowned. I shook my head and looked away, but she shouted again. And again. It wasn't until Kitty threw the truck into reverse that Jess's voice finally penetrated.

Read it, Shauna.

Read what? My phone had no messages. She hadn't given me anything in school. But Jess did know my locker combination. She used to help herself to my stuff all the time. As Kitty peeled from the parking lot to get away from our once-upon-a-time friend, I started digging through my bag. Jess was bad at things like *boundaries* and *personal space*. Why would that change now that we weren't friends?

It only took a minute for me to find the photocopied pages held together by a red paper clip. They were wedged into my English textbook between the cover and the first page. She'd written a note across the back in her familiar hen scratch:

Her last letter was dated the day before her death certificate. This was written the next day. How did Mary die?

October 30, 1864

Mrs. Simpson,

It is with sincere regret that I write you bearing more bad news. I returned from my evening walk to find your sister missing from the church. She must have snuck off before dinnertime. The constable has been informed, but thus far there is no trace of her. It is as if Mary were plucked from us by the hand of God.

I am sorry. I know how upsetting this must be to read.

I bear no ill will toward your sister, so please understand that the things I put to page are for the purposes of enlightenment, not slander. Your sister was rather angry that she could not join you in Boston after your mother's passing. However, the constable and I agreed that she was better served taking refuge in the church until your husband could collect her. She is a virtuous girl, and comely, too. Allowing her to travel unchaperoned would have left her vulnerable to the world's atrocities. My conscience would not abide such endangerment.

I explained this to Mary, assuring her that Mr. Simpson would arrive upon the birth of your baby, but she struggled against reason. She has been increasingly agitated since your mother's death. Doctor Whitten concluded her uncharacteristic aggression was a manifestation of grief. He suggested hospitalization and a steady dose of laudanum, but I respectfully declined. This is a spiritual malady, not a physical one. There is nothing wrong with her that cannot be cured by the firm yet loving hand of our Lord.

We had begun to traverse the path of holy rehabilitation before she disappeared. She continued to fight my influence, questioning my motives and accusing me of unnecessary cruelty. I do not know how your mother raised her, but I modeled my guardianship after Proverbs 13:24:

> Whoever spared the rod hates their children,
> But the one who loves their children
> is careful to discipline them.

I would not brook her caustic demeanor, nor would I "leave her alone" as she so vehemently demanded. Her insistence only steeled my resolve to see her righted. Given time and a modicum of agreeability on your sister's part, I believe we could have eradicated her discord. She could have lived the life of peace and goodness that God intended.

It is my earnest hope that we find her soon so this can still come to pass.

I met with the constable before writing you, and we are in accord that Mary has fled Solomon's Folly. This alarms me for many reasons, not the least of which is her decline. No matter what she may believe, I wish for nothing to befall the girl. Perhaps Mary will find her way to your doorstep before this letter does. Should that occur, please write to me at once. I am sick with concern.

I pray for you and yours, Mrs. Simpson.

Your humble servant,

Philip Starkcrowe

Pastor, Southbridge Parish

2

I read the letter aloud during the drive to Kitty's house. Her color rose the more I talked, pink tinging her cheeks and the tips of her ears. Her hands throttled the steering wheel.

"He beat her," Kitty said. "That's what I'm hearing."

"It sounds like it." I reread the scripture passage, my jaw clenching. "The more I learn about Philip Starkcrowe, the more I think he killed her. I guess she could have run away, but it seems too convenient after everything he put her through."

Kitty nodded. "Exactly. And when would she have had the chance? He locked her in the basement, for crying out loud."

After what Mary did to me, Anna, and Bronx, I swore I'd never feel sorry for her, but the more story we uncovered, the more my stance softened. If anyone had the right to rise as an angry ghost, it was Mary Worth.

Silence filled the car. I wrestled with my conflicting emotions while Kitty drove. She looked angry. The letter was upsetting, but it shouldn't have been enough to get her red-faced and stiff.

"You okay?" I reached out to tap her leg. "You look ready to explode."

"It feels like Jess is trying to lure us into working with her. Like, was this bait? Where the hell is she getting all this stuff?"

"Probably the same place she got the first four letters." I stuffed the newest letter into the notebook. "Jess never said specifically, but with her relation to Mary, I wouldn't doubt if there are family archives. A relative or something."

Kitty's fingers relaxed on the wheel. "As long as we're on the same page. I'm not helping her, Shauna. I won't be bribed with information."

"That's fine. Did you see that cut on her face? Mary got her good."

Kitty shrugged, but I could tell by the faint lines at the sides of her eyes that she wasn't as aloof as she wanted to appear. "If you don't want to get attacked by a ghost, don't summon one."

That was the gist of it, wasn't it?

I thought about the question Jess wrote on the back of the letter. Mary Worth's death certificate listed a date of death but no cause. If Mary ran away from home, it was possible she wasn't interred in the Southbridge Parish as we initially suspected. We knew about the church from Mary's letters, which is how we ended up on a Saturday night descending into a dark, cold basement better suited for the bats than teenaged girls. We had just found a dip in the floor when Mary appeared, cutting the investigation short.

We said we'd go back, but we hadn't. Not yet, anyway. Our research was limited to books and movies. Unfortunately, everything we read about "real hauntings" talked about the history of famous hauntings, not what to do when a murderous ghost tailed you. We were left with theatrics for inspiration, where the haunted heroes always did one of three things: solved the mystery of the ghost's death, found the body and lit it on fire, or rediscovered a prized possession tying the ghost to the mortal plane.

"Hopefully finding her tomb will help us figure out what to do next," I said, my fingers worrying the corners of the letter poking up from the notebook top.

"Then what?"

"Destroy the body, I guess."

Kitty winced. "Gross. I guess it's fine as long as we don't have to deal with Jess or actually touch dead people."

Kitty seemed different since Mary. She'd always been the soft one in our quartet—too pliant when Jess made demands, unwilling to stand up for herself when it mattered most. The haunting changed her. Or maybe it only seemed that way because she used to be with Anna all the time and I was with Jess. Now that we hung out constantly, Kitty's quiet steel was more evident. Her determination to see Mary stopped. The way she picked herself up off the floor after a particularly sad day. I couldn't help but think I'd underestimated her all along. Kitty had known the risks of summoning Mary that last time, but she'd done it anyway to save me.

That was brave. Stupid, but brave.

"We'll stay away from Jess," I promised. "And I'll text Cody later about the letter. She'll have some input."

Cody Jackson was a thirty-something-year-old woman who lived in Mary Worth's hometown of Solomon's Folly. She was also the victim before me. For seventeen years, Mary tormented Cody. Mary took Cody's eye and several fingers and toes. She scratched Cody so badly, Cody looked like she'd wrestled an alligator.

Yet Cody survived, living in squalor to keep the ghost at bay. There was no glass in her house. No shiny plastic or metal. She never went outside. She'd painted her walls and window-panes with pig's blood to stop Mary from tracking her scent. The experience had left her an anxious, surly mess. But I liked her quirks. We talked at least three times a week. She'd invited us to stay with her during the summer break so we could inves-tigate Mary.

Mom had approved the trip, though she thought I was visit-ing Jess's grandparents. I'd vacationed with Jess's family since my Girl Scout days—canoeing, bonfires, horseshoes, and bar-becues by the lake. I didn't like lying to my mother, but she'd never allow me to stay with Cody, a woman she'd never met. It didn't help that Cody was twitchier than a hair dryer in the bathtub, so introductions were off the table. Mom would have steered me clear of someone so strange.

Cody's house stinking of pig's blood. Clouds of flies covering the ceiling. Black paper on the windows. No mirrors, no glass, no reflections. Scars on the skin. Scars on the soul. Fear the only constant companion.

Mom had no idea how close to that I'd come.

We pulled into Kitty's driveway, me clutching my book bag to my chest, Kitty quiet and broody. I cleared my throat. "I'm wondering if we should bother visiting the church again. A hole in the basement floor isn't a lot to go on," I said. "The pastor could be lying in the letter, but remember what Mary wrote about Elizabeth Hawthorne taunting her through the door? People would have heard shouting." I climbed from the car and followed Kitty to the side door. Her father's wealth meant they could afford things like a Jacuzzi near the in-ground pool and summer-only cars. The first floor of their house could fit my rinky-dink apartment four times over.

Kitty unlocked the door and dropped her purse in the foyer. "Yeah, but the pastor could have gagged her and tied her up so no one could hear her cry out. I think it's worth a visit."

I shuddered. Kitty hadn't been at the church with us. I'd given her all the gritty details, but she hadn't experienced Mary lunging up from that dark water. She hadn't seen Mary reaching for me.

Cold, dead hands, her skin rubbery and slick. Fingers curling around my ankles, nails puncturing my skin. Mary jerking me into the water, my head nearly crashing against the steps on the way down. Mary's fist in my hair, shoving me down, down, down, until I saw black.

"Shauna? Are you okay?"

Kitty's voice tore me from the memory. I blinked, as if I could force the image away. As if it wasn't eternally burned into my mind.

"Sorry. I just...yeah. I hate the church."

"I know. Maybe Cody and I can go for you. You can stay at the house."

Kitty and I exchanged glances. I didn't say anything because I didn't have to. We were in it together, for better or worse.

⁂

"Dinner, kiddo!"

Mom picked me up from Kitty's at half past five. We were home by quarter of six, me disappearing into my room, Mom foraging in the kitchen for food. It was almost seven when she called out for dinner, interrupting my studying. I'd been attempting—and failing—to concentrate on my history final. Starkcrowe's letter chewed on my brain. I'd left a message for Cody, but she hadn't called me back yet. Cody liked to do things on her own timetable.

I put aside the book and rolled off my bed. My room was different post-Mary; I'd packed the vanity mirror in the closet and faced it toward the wall. Jess had told me that people once covered their mirrors in the presence of the dying so their souls wouldn't get trapped. With all I'd seen with Bloody Mary, a vanity was nightmare fodder I didn't need.

I trudged down the hall in my pajamas, keeping to the middle to avoid the bathroom on the left and the picture frames on the right. Mom stood by the kitchen table, doling out canned beef stew. She smiled as I sat. She looked better these days—less tired now that she worked sixty hours instead of eighty.

Perfect skin, rich auburn hair. Her eyes were too big, her nose too narrow, her mouth too wide, but together, the parts worked. She was beautiful. I had enough of my dad in me that I didn't come together so well, with pointier features and a wider jaw. Plus, I had the redhead's plague. Freckles.

"How's studying going?" she asked, sliding into the chair across from me. She stretched her napkin over her lap.

"Okay." I paused to think of something normal to say. "I think I bombed the calculus final."

Mom frowned for a moment, then forced a shrug. "You had a good-enough quarter otherwise. One test shouldn't matter too much."

Mom was usually all over me for grades. I was an honor roll kid, Ivy League material without Ivy League money. I needed a scholarship if I wanted to go somewhere great. But after Anna died, Mom eased up on expectations. I was sure she thought I was crazy, the way my eyes swept through every room looking for spooks and shadows. The way I pressed into her side whenever the lights were dim.

"Yeah, thanks." My spoon dipped into the gray, murky stew with bits of carrot floating in it.

We fell into awkward silence. Our post-Anna lives had taken on an awful routine. Extended quiet followed by Mom asking, "Are you okay?" "How can I help?" and "Do you want to talk to a professional?"

"I have a date on Friday," she announced instead.

My spoon clattered against the edge of the bowl.

"Seriously?"

"Yes, *seriously*. It's not that strange, is it? I'm not a hundred, you know."

Not strange, but unexpected. It'd always been just me and Mom—my dad walked out on us when I was four. He could be dead, for all I know. The notion of her playing the field again was . . . well, it wasn't bad, but it wasn't familiar.

"It's fine. I'm fine," I lied.

Splotchy hives dotted her pale neck, telegraphing her embarrassment. "His name is Scott. He's an electrician. He came into McReady's a few months ago. I've been turning him down ever since, but I think I might like him. He's funny."

"I hope you have an awesome time," I said after a minute.

She nodded.

Back to the silence.

Every few bites she glanced at me, hopeful I'd have something to say about *anything*. Her date. My day. My finals. I used to chitchat, but I'd become so consumed with Mary that I had nothing to contribute to the conversations anymore.

For the first time in a long time, I asked myself why I continued to keep Mary quiet. Fear, yes, but fear of what? Being doubted? Jess had convinced us that no one would believe it. That we'd be called liars. She used Elsa Samburg's institutionalization as the worst-case scenario. Elsa was another Mary victim, older than Cody, who'd been hospitalized after her haunting.

But my mom knew I wasn't prone to hysteria. I didn't watch

horror movies or believe in UFOs or yetis. I didn't read horoscopes or tarot cards. And I definitely didn't make up stories for attention.

"Do you believe in ghosts?" I asked.

Mom's spoon paused midway between her mouth and the bowl. She blinked at me, surprise evident in the lift of her brows. "I don't know, really. Your grandmother does. She thinks her room at the rest home is haunted."

"I was haunted. I know how stupid it sounds, but it's true. For real." I had to get it all out before I lost my courage. "That's why I've been so twitchy. I swear I'm not crazy. This isn't because of Anna. It happened before Anna and it's over now, but that week was awful."

She put down her spoon and stared at me. She didn't look afraid, just incredulous that her reasonable daughter said such an unreasonable thing.

"I didn't tell you because I was afraid you'd look exactly how you look right now," I said. "I was scared. And please don't give me the stuff about logical explanations. It was a ghost of a girl named Mary Worth, who died a hundred and fifty years ago."

Mom's mouth opened as if she was about to say something. She bit her bottom lip instead, leaving a wet smear. "I see. Well, no, I don't, but...you're not haunted anymore?"

"No. It's over. I know how insane this is, but I would really like for you to give me the benefit of the doubt. I swear it happened. Please."

I didn't realize how desperate I was for her not to turn her back on me until I heard the plaintive *please*. She heard it, too; she nodded and retrieved her spoon, turning it over in her hand. "You're safe?" she asked.

"I am now."

Mom took a bite of stew and glanced from me to the table-cloth, her brow covered in worry lines. The silence chiseled away at my confidence. I'd overestimated. Jess knew what she was talking about. Confessing to something a month old was needless and stupid and...

Mom's gaze locked with mine. "I believe you."

3

Those three words were magical. I'd shaken off a shackle that had weighed me down more than I'd realized. I looked away, my fingers curling along the edge of the table, my eyes teary with relief.

"Thanks." The lump in my throat felt like a softball. "I was afraid you'd laugh at me."

Mom reached across the table to take my hand, her fingers warm around my wrist. "I've never done that in seventeen years, Shauna. I'm not going to start now."

The questions started, though Mom was gentle. She knew how fragile the trust I'd laid upon her doorstep was. "Who was Mary Worth?" "How'd you find out about her?" "What happened when you were haunted?" I never mentioned Bloody Mary by name, mirrors, Anna's fate, or Solomon's Folly, but I did talk about what Mary looked like. I talked about how I suspected she died. I shared a version of the truth that was palatable for both of us, and more important, allowed me to go to Solomon's Folly. If Mom suspected I'd be ghost hunting, the trip would be off the table.

We sat together in the living room, staring at the TV with pillows hugged to our chests. The floor above us creaked, a rusty squeal. I tensed, but then water rushed and pipes shivered. The toilet. It wasn't phantoms or ghouls, just regular people doing regular things. I let out my breath.

"Are you still scared of the ghost?" Mom must have been watching me from the corner of her eye. I shifted my weight, trying not to squirm too much.

"Sometimes," I admitted. "But it's getting easier as time goes on."

There was another pause. "I hate to ask this, but you're not doing anything weird? No séances or witchcraft?"

I flinched. That question was one of the reasons I didn't want to say anything to begin with. "God, Mom. No." I stood up to go back to my room, but she snatched my wrist and squeezed.

"Sorry. I believe you. It's the worry talking."

I wrenched my hand away and retraced my steps to my bedroom, the door slamming behind me.

She doesn't believe me.

My fingers went to my temples, attempting to massage away the brewing headache. Mary, Mom's date, Solomon's Folly, Jess. I was supposed to study, but how could I focus with so much noise in my head?

A nap. I needed a nap. I threw myself into bed, pinching

my eyes closed. Except there were footsteps approaching and a swift knock on my door and *why couldn't she just leave me alone*?

"Shauna? Hey." Mom poked her head in, her hands clutching the door. "I'm sorry. Oh, hon. I didn't mean to upset you."

But you did. Now go away.

I rolled away from her. "Thanks, Mom. Love you."

Her breath hitched. "I love you, too. I'm heading in to read before bed. If you need anything, let me know. I don't know much about ghosts, but if you say you're safe now, I'm ... I have to believe you. You know I'm here."

I stumbled through school the next morning, my head low. There was only English left to survive before I could eat lunch with Kitty. Some of my classmates said hello as I passed, but I wouldn't look up at them. A wall of windows lined my left side. So shiny and tall. So menacing.

Running down the hall, Mary keeping pace no matter how hard I pumped my legs. That awful grin. That obscene laughter. Six Marys in the panes, all mocking me, the cackles ringing out like a chorus from Hell. Reflection upon reflection delighting in my fear. Skidding around the corner to find a hallway of locks clanging against metal lockers. BANG, BANG, BANG!

Mary had become part of the school. Every mirror, every chrome knob, every darkened corner. She was my ever-present shadow. I rushed to my locker to get my books for the next class, dancing with nervous energy. A hand clapped my shoulder from behind. I shrieked, instinctively reaching for the box of salt hidden beneath my gym clothes. My elbow jerked back, colliding with a warm, hard body.

The hand plunging through the glass. Nails rending flesh, blood rising hot and thick and smelling like copper. Mud and the stench of decay as she heaves herself across the glass barrier. Snarling, her upper lip curved, a tendril of yellow spittle dribbling down her chin. The slits of nostrils flaring as she catches her prey's scent.

"Holy crap! Shauna, sorry, you okay? Ow. Damn."

I whipped my head around. Standing there, her hand hovering midair, was Laurie Carmichael. Spiky black hair, brown eyes, a pink-glossed smile. Laurie was one of those girls that everyone liked—she played a lot of sports, was involved in a lot of clubs. She could be fake at times, and she had a tendency to gossip, but she'd never aimed any of it my way, so I didn't have too much of a problem with her.

Especially since she'd been one of the girls to help Jess in that last summoning. She and I shared a secret—something we'd probably never bring up to one another, but we both knew it was there. That meant something.

I eased away from the salt.

"I'm so sorry. You scared me. Are you okay?"

Laurie rubbed at her shoulder. "Yeah, I'll be fine. But take it easy, girl. Damn. Anyway, I wanted to let you know I'm having an end-of-the-year party Friday. You're invited. I already mentioned it to Kitty."

I said nothing at first, fumbling for a response that didn't sound dismissive or bitchy. "I'm not all that social with the Anna thing going on. Is Jess going?"

"No. I haven't seen her much since her breakup with Marc. How about you?"

I didn't know Jess and Marc had split. I had to wonder if she'd ditched him to protect him from Mary.

Maybe if I'd dumped my friends like Cody told me to do, Anna would still be here. How can Jess be a better person than me?

"No. We're not talking," I said tightly.

Laurie looked like she wanted to hear more. I turned back to my locker, not ignoring her but not inviting a second degree either. She stepped away with a sigh. "Yeah, okay, that's fair. Eight o'clock if you change your mind. Invitation's open to the whole class."

"Thanks." My voice was hollow, even to my ears.

"Maybe it'll be fun," Kitty said.

I picked at my food, my eyes scanning the cafeteria. I was looking for Jess. After the car incident the day before, I expected to find her staring at me, but no—when I spotted her, she was concentrating on a notebook. She had a bandage on her face and her hair was chopped short above her ears. Even from that distance, I could see bruises around her throat. I wondered if the teachers suspected Jess's parents of abuse.

"She looks like shit," I said, motioning with my fork. Kitty looked to see where I was pointing and grunted.

"She does. Shauna, you're not thinking of..."

"What? No."

"Good."

I glanced over at Jess to see her gathering her notebook to her chest and racing out of the cafeteria. A month ago, she was surrounded by people, the popular girl. The shining star and homecoming queen and everything high-school dreams were made of. Now, she was a shadow. No people, no prospects, no *hope*.

I'm not that girl anymore. I'm alive. I'm unhaunted.

Some things remained untainted by Mary. Parties at the end of junior year were one of those things.

"Okay," I said, looking back to Kitty. "We'll go."

4

"It's Cody. What do you need?"

Cody never opened her calls with a "Hi" or "Hello." She just announced herself with that deep, raspy voice that sometimes fell to a whisper midsentence. She sounded like she'd gargled with lit charcoals, but that was bound to happen when you didn't talk for almost a decade. Even after a month of regular conversation, her voice hadn't recovered.

I had to strain to hear her, but it was a small price to pay. Cody could be tough to handle with the paranoia and mood swings, but she was also my friend. She'd risked her neck to talk to me during my haunting. Her tips kept me alive.

If I'd listened more, they would have kept Anna alive, too.

I read her the letter from Starkcrowe to Constance after Mary's disappearance, pausing to repeat certain sentences when she asked me to.

"Starkcrowe doesn't deny manhandling Mary." Cody's voice

rose and fell on a wave. "It's not hard to imagine the abuse getting out of control. I can't...I don't—" She grumbled beneath her breath, something I couldn't quite make out over the phone line. "We need to find out what he did to her."

"That's been the goal all along." I threw myself into the chair in my room and smoothed the letter out over the armrest. "But we don't have much to go on."

"We have the letters. And the church is significant. What about that dip in the floor you told me about?"

"What about it?"

"It's possible there's something under there. Or maybe there's a grave marker somewhere on the property. If she's buried with Hannah, that would complicate things, but it can't hurt to look."

Hannah's suicide meant she would have been denied a Christian burial. Mary didn't believe Hannah had leapt to her death in the river, but that didn't stop the pastor from having Hannah interred somewhere other than the parish.

"Okay. If there's anything I can do before the weekend, let me know. We're going to a party Friday night but should be coming out on Saturday," I said.

"You're useless to me. Not your fault, but that's the trouble with being seventeen. You're limited. I'll buy the supplies." Cody sucked in a deep breath before blowing it right onto the receiver and nearly blasting out my eardrum. "I'm assuming Jess is not invited? I don't want her around. She's a risk, and she pisses me off."

I eyed Kitty, who lay on her bed texting Bronx. "No, we're

not bringing Jess. We've seen her at school, but we haven't talked to her. It doesn't look like she's escaped Mary."

Kitty wouldn't look at me, shaking her head in disgust and continuing her text.

Cody snorted. "Not surprising. She probably won't be able to pass her off on her own. It's easier to choreograph a haunting when you're not the focus. Mary's chaotic. Too many things can go wrong."

I sat up straighter in my chair, moving the phone over to my other ear. "What do you mean? She tried to tag Kitty for me. It's feasible."

"Feasible, yes. Smart, no. Not when you're the prey. With a fresh summon, any of the four girls are potential victims. Jess had a clear advantage over the rest of you. She knew how to avoid Mary. I bet she kept herself farthest away from the mirror when you summoned, right?"

"Right."

Cody continued, talking so fast it was hard to understand her. "But now, if she summons Mary, Mary is gunning for her. She wants Jess's blood. Jess knows that. It's too risky. Being the farthest from the mirror isn't enough anymore."

"But Mary *has* hurt other people when she already has a target."

"Of course she has, but think of it this way—of all the times Mary showed up in your reflection, how many times was she interested in other people? Sometimes, but not always, right? How willing were you to summon Mary when you were haunted?"

"I didn't want to. It terrified me," I said.

"Exactly."

Kitty sat up on the bed behind me. She reached out to touch my hair, her fingers twining in the strands and braiding. The gentle tug on my scalp felt nice.

I slumped into my seat, eyes going half-mast like a cat in sunlight. "I'm so sick of Mary. Hopefully we can finish this soon."

"Agreed. Stay safe." The line went dead against my ear. No *good-bye* or *talk to you soon*—Cody was just gone.

∞

The days blurred one into the next: school, Kitty's house, home, Mom, studying, bed. I managed to stay on the honor roll for the last term, but barely. I cleaned out my locker the last day of classes, flinching every time metal clashed with metal or the door to the bathroom across the hall opened and closed. I couldn't wait to escape that building. Every turn was a bad memory.

Steam from the showers. Swampy water rising from the drains, putrid and nestling in the grout between the floor tiles. The showerheads burping filthy water into the fiberglass stalls. The three of us sloshing in it, sliding in it. Feet burning. Sweat rising. Mary laughing from the fog before the strike. Tearing Anna from my grasp. Drag, drag, dragging. The mirror closing behind her. Blood splashing across the glass.

"Get me out, get me out, get me out," I whispered.

I threw the remaining papers into the trash bin, grabbed

my book bag, and slammed the locker closed, my jaw clenching at the rattle. I passed the janitor's closet where Bronx, Mrs. Reyes, and I hid when Mary put the school in lockdown. All those chrome locks slamming against the lockers had sounded like gunshots.

Helicopters, emergency protocol, a media storm. It was a disaster.

I spotted Kitty outside the principal's office, gazing at the student-made memorial for Anna. After the disappearance, people left wreaths, flowers, and teddy bears along the football field fence—so many they'd wrapped around both sides and wound down to the soccer field. Someone had preserved some of the smaller mementos, along with Anna's school picture, yearbook photos, and some sympathy cards.

Kitty's hand touched the display case, tears streaming down her cheeks.

"I feel like I'm abandoning her. I don't know why I assume she's here, but I do. So leaving for the summer..." She couldn't finish the thought. I slung an arm around her shoulders and pulled her close. She dropped her head onto my shoulder and cried. Heartrending sobs that devolved into wheezy, asthmatic coughs.

My eyes skimmed the pictures on the board. Some were from class trips, others from the candid section in the yearbook. The one at the center was Anna on the tennis team, wearing her short shorts and holding a racket. Anna played only freshman year and she hated it, but it was a good solo shot, her head turned to the side, her lips tipped up into a smile. Her black hair was back in a ponytail, the glasses on her nose glinting in the sun.

Emptiness crept into my gut. Not the kind that suggested emotional numbness, but the kind that said I desperately needed something to fill the space her loss left inside of me.

I miss my friend.

We lingered awhile, my eyes stinging with unshed tears, Kitty taking hits off her inhaler. She was purple in the face and shaking. Eventually, I guided her away from the display and toward the parking lot.

"Do you want me to drive?" I offered.

She shook her head and climbed into the driver's side of her car, flinging her book bag behind her. It exploded in a flurry of paper and clutter.

Kitty checked her reflection in the rearview mirror, dashing at the mascara tracks raining down her cheeks. I tensed beside her. One of us had reconciled her relationship with mirrors. It wasn't me.

Mary in Jess's car windows, surrounding us, her fingers curled over into meat hooks as she lashed from the depths of the glass. Her visage shifting to the windshield, the ghost looking like a big, dead hood ornament. Raising that finger to write a single word across the condensation on the window. SHAUNA. My name. Staking her claim with a hissed litany of "Mine, mine, mine..."

"Glad we've got a few hours before the party," Kitty said.

"Yeah. Yes," I stammered.

The high school shrunk as Kitty drove away from the parking lot. I didn't share Kitty's fear that we were leaving Anna behind—not when I knew that Mary's world could be reached through any mirror anywhere. Anna wasn't in the locker room. Anna was in that swamp with the rest of Mary's victims. Sometimes I tried reasoning out where that was exactly—Ghost World, Purgatory, Hell. Wherever it was, I never wanted to see it.

The drive was silent, Kitty and I lost to our private burdens. I remembered to text Mom to let her know I'd be staying at Kitty's overnight. Her *have fun* reply popped up right as Kitty pulled into her driveway. Instead of climbing out, she tilted her head back so she could look out the skylight, her eyes still swollen from crying at the school.

"Do you still want to go?" she asked.

"I thought you wanted to."

There was a long pause before she nodded and climbed out of her car. "I think *something* needs to make my bad feelings go away."

Seeing the strain around her eyes and the slight jut of her chin, I was pretty sure she needed it, too.

5

Laurie's house was off of a side street, making it the perfect location for a party—no streetlights, long distances between houses. It was one story, baby blue, with a deck, a porch swing, and potted plants dangling from the roof overhang. The windows were open, the screen door propped with a garden gnome to let air in and music out. I could hear the dance track the moment I stepped out of the SUV.

People talked in clusters around the front and side lawns. "Bronx said to take pictures," Kitty said. Before I could escape, she kissed my cheek and snapped a selfie. The flash blinded me—white lightning burned into my eyeballs.

The world shifted into focus once we entered the house. We were in a kitchen with half a dozen kids talking in front of the sink. Within ten seconds, I knew every reflective surface within arm's reach: the dishwasher, the refrigerator, the faucets, the window facing the backyard. I stiffened seeing my reflection staring back at me from the glass sliding doors. My hands reached into my pocket for my Tic Tac container of salt.

Just in case.

Laurie Carmichael separated herself from the kitchen pack. She'd dressed up for the party, all cute blouse and skirt, her makeup perfect, her shoes too shiny to be anything but new. I'd barely taken the time to brush my hair and put on ChapStick before coming out. Kitty cared more about her look, but not by much. Our standards were a lot lower than they used to be.

Laurie motioned us farther into the house, through a living room with a flat-screen TV and past five kids piled on the couch. Down the hall, a bathroom to my left, a closed door to my right, until we entered a study with dark paint and darker wooden floors. Bookshelves lined an entire wall. A desk with a computer was nestled into the corner. A black leather couch with a glass coffee table occupied the bulk of the room. I eyed the table suspiciously, briefly glancing at the squat stone fertility statue at the center.

"Bags on the couch if you want. Glad you could make it," Laurie said. "I know it's been hard for you guys."

"Thanks, Laurie." Kitty smiled at her. Laurie patted her on the shoulder and ducked back into the hall to welcome more guests.

Kitty put her coat, purse, and sweatshirt on the pile. She checked her reflection in the glass of the coffee table, patting her hair into place. I flinched for her. She caught it, and her eyes drifted from me to the table before she backed into the hall.

"I forget sometimes," she said.

How?

We rejoined the party. Waves, hugs. Nathan O'Donnell nodded at me. Nathan and I went out last year, after Jess convinced me he was cool. He spent the whole date talking about sports and video games. I rebuffed his late-date groping attempts. Jess had given me grief for it, saying I didn't give him a fair chance, that I'd "put her in an awkward position" because he was friends with her boyfriend.

So many things I should have seen about Jess early on—so many symptoms that she was too selfish to be a good friend.

Kitty floated through the room, telling everyone to smile for Bronx before subjecting them to her camera. I watched her, jealous that she could go so quickly from sadness to functional and pleasant. And happy. I hadn't experienced happy in what felt like forever.

Every time someone wandered to the bathroom, they nodded at me like it was their solemn duty to acknowledge the grieving girl in the corner. I followed Kitty wherever she drifted, but I wasn't being part of the event. I watched the people around me as if they were specimens in a laboratory.

I was, for a time, the ghost in the room.

A keg rolled in at half past eight courtesy of the football team. There was dancing, spin the bottle, drinking games played at the picnic table out back. I volunteered to be the designated driver, so I kept to soda, but Kitty started drinking almost right away. I figured she deserved to forget. If I thought it'd help me put Mary behind me, I would have been right there with her, but what if it made everything worse? I couldn't allow myself to lose control. I kept to myself, my thumb rubbing circles across the lid of the Tic Tac box.

An hour passed and then two, everything growing louder. More kids dancing. Kids yelling. Kids making out in dimly lit corners. I stayed on the fringes, Kitty always close.

Then Jess arrived.

I was near the porch, one eye on the windows, the other on Kitty as she played another round of quarters. Jess's green car pulled up onto the edge of the lawn and she launched herself from the driver's seat. She spun around, throwing something at the car before sprinting toward the house.

Get out. Get out. Get out. Get Kitty and get out.

I ducked around the corner of the house, hoping Jess wouldn't see me, but it was too late. As I reached Kitty to pull her away from the table games, Jess called my name. My hand clapped on Kitty's shoulder. She lifted her head and smiled until she saw my expression.

"What's wrong?"

"Jess." Even drunk, Kitty knew what that meant. She followed my lead, her sandal getting caught in the grass. I reached out to steady her, letting her sag into my side as we rushed back to the house.

Jess chased us inside, winded, her cheeks apple red.

"Wait. Guys. Please," she said, her voice cracking.

"I can't, Jess. I'm sorry."

I moved quickly. Past the kids on the couch, down the hall, and into the side office with the purses and coats. Kitty broke away to paw through the pile, swaying dangerously on her feet. I heard movement in the hall and then Jess was there, her hands braced against the doorway. "Wait, both of you. Please!" Jess grabbed my shoulder, her fingers digging in and punishing.

I jerked away. "Stop, please!"

"Go home, Jess," Kitty snapped. "You'll get everyone killed."

"I needed to be around friends. It's my parents' anniversary and they left me with Todd. It was the two of us. Mary came. I can't let her take my brother. So I left him with our neighbor, Mrs. Downey. Please."

I'd known Todd since he was born eight years ago. He could be annoying, but he was a good kid. He loved Matchbox cars and SpongeBob and LEGO. He didn't deserve to be sliced up by Jess's terrible shadow.

"Let's go," Kitty barked. "I'm not staying here." I knew she was right, but I hesitated all the same, glancing between Kitty and Jess. Just weeks ago, we'd all been friends.

It's Jess's fault. You can't shoulder this. Go to Solomon's Folly tomorrow, without Jess.

"Shauna, please!" The desperation in Jess's voice was palpable, the fear impossible to fake.

"She's dangerous, Shauna," Kitty said. "Let's go!"

My best friend from my past and my best friend from the present. Both wanted opposite things of me, but the decision wasn't hard to make. Jess's betrayal forever tainted what had been a good thing for a lot of years. I offered my hand to Kitty, my jaw clenched. I couldn't shake the feeling that turning my back on Jess was her death sentence.

If Mary kills us before we solve her murder, Jess is screwed anyway. Save Kitty. Save yourself. Get away from the haunted girl before something else goes horribly wrong.

"We're leaving," I said.

Kitty staggered my way, the alcohol robbing her of her grace. I reached out to help her, my hand cupping her elbow, when she tumbled to the floor in front of me. I thought it was the beer, but then I realized it was something much, much worse. The sickening smell of overripe fruit and brine water filled the room.

Only one thing had that foul tang—that stench of rot and death.

Mary.

My heart pounded faster than a hummingbird's wing. I couldn't see Mary, I could only see Kitty's expression and the purse flying from her grasp. I reached for Kitty, hugging her chest to mine and wrapping my arms around her waist. I wouldn't lose anyone else to the ghost. I'd anchor Kitty to the world with my weight, and if not that, I'd go wherever Mary dragged us.

Kitty's panicked shrieks punctured my eardrums. Her hands balled up in my sweatshirt as she struggled to hold on.

Mary followed Jess here. Kitty got too close.

I tried to lift her, but something jerked her back and away from me. No, not something. *Someone.* An arm stretched out from the underside of the glass coffee table and wrapped around Kitty's leg. Gray skin, black spidery veins pulsing beneath the surface of the thin flesh. A clawed hand equally as dark save for a single digit that looked cotton-candy pink next to its sisters. A gash splayed open the arm from the inside of the elbow to the wrist, a network of fetid tendons twining around the brittle-looking bones.

Kitty dropped in front of me, Mary wrenching her to the floor. I teetered, nearly falling forward myself, but then Jess was there. White granules flew by my face and toward the arm, but the top of the table protected the ghost below. Eventually, the salt would harden the glass so Mary couldn't pass through, but that took a lot of salt and more time than we had. Jess knew it, too. She grabbed the fertility statue and lifted it over her head. *CRUNCH.* She smashed it down on Mary's elbow. The bones snapped on impact. Mary shrieked from inside the table glass, her voice echoing as if she menaced us from the depths of a cave.

Jess beat Mary's exposed arm, one heavy strike following another. Over and over she pummeled her until Mary relinquished her hold on Kitty's leg. I pulled Kitty to safety as an arc of black blood splashed across Jess's face. Mary's blood. It dribbled down Jess's cheek and stained her blond hair, but she never stopped her onslaught. Not until the ghost pulled her wounded arm back into the rippling depths of the table.

"Get out," Jess said, her voice oddly flat.

I didn't reply. I couldn't. Fear filled my mouth and throat like liquid, drowning any words I may have wanted to say. Kitty hauled herself to her feet to stumble from the room. Finding the hallway barred by curious classmates, she screeched at them to move.

Jess reached into her coat and pulled out a box of salt,

spraying the top of the table in a thick layer so it'd solidify. "I'm sorry. Tell her I'm sorry. It's my fault. Again," she said.

"Go home," I rasped. "There's too much glass here. You're going to get someone else killed."

I snagged Kitty's purse and ran. Tried to run. Kids lined the hall, their eyes huge. I didn't know if any of them had seen Mary. Right then, I didn't care. I had to get away. I'd made a lot of promises about saving innocents from the ghost, but faced with Mary again, all I could do was flee.

6

"Did she cut you?" I asked over Kitty's hysterical sobbing. She didn't answer. I gripped the steering wheel harder. *"KITTY. Did Mary cut you? Did she break the skin?"*

"I don't think so!" she wailed, sucking in a breath and diving for the inhaler in her purse. She fumbled, and it fell into the well between the seats. I rummaged for it, only one eye on the road, and managed to retrieve it without driving us into a tree.

Kitty breathed in from the inhaler as if it was her lifeline, but the moment it was out of her mouth, she slapped at the car's window.

"Pull over," she croaked. I eased the SUV onto the curb. Kitty threw open the door and staggered into the tall grass, doubling over at the waist before collapsing to the ground.

I unbuckled my seat belt and let myself out of the car to help her.

"Why'd Jess come?" Kitty asked. She lifted swollen eyes to me, her face pale, burst blood vessels riddling her cheeks. I looped my arm around her waist and guided her back into the car, careful where I put my feet.

"She was scared for Todd," I said. "Mary showed up, and she had to bring him to the neighbor's house."

"But why'd she come to the party?"

"She wanted her friends. Mary doesn't like crowds. I don't know, and I'm not sure it matters." The mistake *we'd* made was going into that side room. We would have been safe if we'd stayed with our classmates.

Stupid, Shauna. Stupid.

I helped buckle Kitty into her seat. Her eyes swept the windows around her, searching for Mary in the blackened shine. I reached into my hoodie and produced the Tic Tac box with the salt, cramming it into Kitty's fist. She stared at it stupidly, but then nodded, wrapping her fingers around it.

We pulled into Kitty's driveway at just after eleven, terrified her father would be waiting. Mr. Almeida wasn't the nicest guy under the best circumstances. Under the worst, he was a bully and a screamer. The darkened windows and closed front door meant we stood a chance of getting in undetected.

I helped Kitty inside, trying to make as little noise as possible on the way up the stairs. Kitty sniffled and whimpered, but I didn't begrudge her the fear. I suffered, too. I just hid it better than she did. Around the corner, down the hall, and into her room. I eased her onto her bed before dropping to my knees and rolling up her pant legs.

"What are you doing?"

"Looking for lacerations." I was pretty sure Mary hadn't caught Kitty's blood scent, or we would have seen her already, but I needed to check. I pulled off Kitty's socks and shoes and rolled her feet around.

No claw marks. My shoulders sagged with relief.

"You're okay," I said.

"No marks?"

"None." I crawled to Kitty's bureau, rifling through the bottom drawer for pajamas. As I pulled out a tank top and a pair of pants, my cell phone beeped in my pocket. I tossed the clothes onto Kitty's bed. "Do you need help getting dressed? If not I'll go see who this is. It might be Mom. Or Cody."

Or Jess.

Kitty nodded and reached for the tank top. I ducked from the room, the phone already in my hand as I shut the door. *Please call,* Jess wrote. I started texting back, but then dialed instead. A short conversation would take twice as long in text.

One ring in, Jess picked up.

"Thank you for calling."

"Hey, how are you?" It slipped out before I remembered I was angry at her.

Old habits.

"Okay? I guess?" Jess sucked in a deep breath. "I have another letter you should see. I'll e-mail it." Something slammed on the other side of the line, and she whined. It was a broken sound, so foreign coming from her. Jess was brazen and confident and fearless.

Or used to be, anyway. Mary stripped everyone to their last nerve.

I walked through Kitty's house and out the front door. The summer peepers were out, screeching their night songs while flutters of moths dove at the front porch light. I watched them, waiting for Jess to collect her thoughts.

"We can beat Mary, Shauna, but if I'm constantly fighting for my life, I can't make headway. I told Aunt Dell what happened. She wants to help, but she's really old and can't do much except share information. She gave me the last few letters. She's lived in Solomon's Folly all her life. With her on our side, we could make this stop for good."

Aunt Dell was Jess's great-aunt and the woman who owned the church where we suspected Mary was buried. I'd never met her in my travels to Solomon's Folly, but Jess had talked about her fondly in the past. She'd called the cops on us the last time we trespassed on her private property, not knowing it was us, but I couldn't be mad at her for it, especially considering the arrival of the police officer saved me from a Mary attack.

Jess went quiet. I could hear rustling on the other side of the line, and then a growl. There was a thud followed by a clatter. "Bitch. You think I don't see you?"

Slam.

I waited. I could hear heavy breathing on the other end of the line, followed by pounding footsteps. A rattle. A hiss. Mary was there with Jess. I would recognize those wet, gurgling groans anywhere. I tensed, clutching the phone. The adrenaline from the party surged again, the hairs on my body prickling.

"Jess?"

"I'm fine," she rasped. "She's contained. The offer stands. You help me, I help you. I'm running out of ideas, Shauna. It's only going to get worse."

I'd shut Jess out after Anna—after the revelation that she'd set us up. After what she tried to do to Kitty to save me. I still didn't want to be her friend, but no one deserved Mary. Not even Jess. She'd done a lot wrong, but she was only seventeen, and seventeen-year-olds weren't supposed to die.

And yet.

My voice wavered. "You had us summon Mary without telling us the real reason you wanted her around, Jess. You never spelled out the dangers. You didn't share half of the information we deserved to know—that people had been hurt. That people had died. Why would you risk your friends like that? Why would you risk me? I was your best friend."

Jess hesitated. I thought she was avoiding the question, but then there was more racket on her end of the line.

Slam. Crack. Squeal.

Jess panted into the receiver. "I didn't want to, Shauna. I didn't. There's so much more to it than that. You don't even know."

Before I could ask what that meant, she hung up.

The text to Jess blinked at me from my phone, my thumb hovering over the SEND button.

Are you okay?

What if Jess took it as an indication that we were fine? Or, worse, what if she didn't answer at all? Would I call her parents? Tell them to check to see if their daughter had gone missing? How would I explain if she was?

I tucked away the phone.

A coward twice in one night, but I had to think about myself. About Kitty. About my mom, and Anna, and everyone else who needed me to get through the Mary gauntlet.

I made my way back to Kitty's bedroom and found her sound asleep. I curled in beside her, watching the alarm clock tick off the hours, rolling over from PM to AM. The dread faded some, but not enough to let me sleep. Then I spied the outline of the Tic Tac box in Kitty's jeans pocket on the floor beside me. I fished it out. The salt calmed my nerves enough that I managed to drift off, but not before I thought about Jess.

Don't be dead. Please don't be dead.

I was angry with her, but I wasn't done caring about her. Kitty wouldn't like that.

A blast of sunshine woke me early—before six on a Saturday. My mother said she wanted to see me before we left for Solomon's Folly. I could have asked Kitty for a ride, but she snored at me from her cocoon of bedding. I scribbled a Post-it note to call me before she picked me up, sticking it to her cell phone so she couldn't miss it.

The walk home helped clear my head. It wasn't hot yet, the last traces of spring dewing the grass and crisping the air. I buried my hands in my hoodie pockets, winding my way around the back roads of Bridgewater. While I wasn't keen on extended exposure to Jess, I didn't want to discount her as an avenue for information. I'd talk to Kitty and Cody about it first, though. Kitty hated Jess more than anything in the world, and Cody didn't trust her. I was the weak link. I was the one who still had memories of sleepovers and Girl Scouts and going to Disney with Jess's family when we were twelve.

I picked up my pace, jogging the rest of the way to the house. I took the front stairs two at a time and unlocked the front door. Unsurprisingly, Mom was awake—she was always an early riser. What *was* surprising was that she was wearing purple lingerie and an open robe making breakfast in the kitchen.

She spun, her eyes huge, a spatula clasped in her left hand. I blinked at her. She blinked at me. She was bare down to her belly button, but she quickly rectified that, bundling up and tossing her spatula aside.

"Shit. Hi, Shauna. Let me..."

"Bonnie? Do you have a spare toothbrush? I didn't think to get—" A tall man with dark hair, a goatee, and green eyes walked from the bathroom and into the living room, his fingers fussing with the fly on his pants. My face colored, and he nearly jumped out of his skin.

"Shauna. This is Scott. I didn't realize you'd be home so soon." Mom's fingers toyed with the dangling belt of the robe. "I would have warned you, but...I'm sorry."

"Yeah, that's...It's cool," I lied. "Kitty was tired and you said you wanted to see me before I left for Solomon's Folly, so I figured I'd walk home."

Mom forced a smile, her attention swinging to Scott. He'd fixed his pants and spun around, palms turned up toward the ceiling.

"Sorry to meet you this way, Shauna. Did you want to have breakfast with us?"

"No. Not really hungry." I glanced at my mother and motioned at the skillet on the stove. "You're smoking." Mom nodded at me. Then nodded again. I gestured at the stove. "Smoking," I repeated.

She clambered for the spatula, maneuvering the bacon around the pan. "Are you sure?" she called out. "There's plenty. Eggs and toast, too."

"No, thanks. I have to pack and shower and stuff." My phone buzzed inside of my pocket. Relieved for the distraction, I pulled it out, expecting it to be Kitty. Instead I saw an e-mail notification from Jess McAllister. The letter. She was alive.

"I should take this," I said weakly.

Mom peered at me from under her brows, mortified. "Sure. We'll talk later."

"That works." I nodded at Scott and took off toward my room.

Darling Constance,

Week three in this place and all I can think of is your smiling face. Your sweet kisses. Your laughter. How is my son? I fear he'll be twice as grown upon my return. If only my business was not so mired in stalemate. Solomon's Folly is not friendly to outsiders seeking justice.

I have twice as many questions as answers.

The pastor of whom your sister wrote took a wife this last week. Elizabeth Hawthorne. She is one of the girls who distressed Mary if I recall my names correctly? It was not a long courtship and I have reason to suspect—if only because of Miss Lucy Chamberlain's rambling monologues—that Miss Hawthorne was ill-prepared for matrimony. According to the baker's daughter, the nuptials came to pass because Mr. Seymour Hawthorne insisted upon the match.

While Miss Chamberlain is not an intellectual, she is pleasant and willing to speak to me. That is more than I can say for her brethren.

(Also, she extends her congratulations on the baby and says she grieves for our family. She has a sweet heart, I think.)

I find the pastor uncooperative. Pleasantries turned sour when I explained why I'd come to The Folly. The constable is not much help either, but at least my warrant got me into the church after Starkcrowe turned me away. It was all rather suspicious; if there was nothing to hide regarding Mary's disappearance, why would the pastor bar me from looking in her bedroom and the church basement? I asked this of the constable. He said the pastor was an old curmudgeon in a young man's clothes.

I wish I had more to report. The basement is every bit as dark as Mary described and infested with beetles. How a man of God could lock a young woman in such a cold, joyless place, I do not know. I had to bring three lanterns down with me. It was sparse: some stacked cartons and a mirror. The floor was disrupted, the bricks askew, which Starkcrowe explained was a result of water and structural damage. I searched it but found no trace of your sister. I do not know if I am relieved or disappointed.

Tomorrow I will explore the river and nearby swamp to find your mother's grave marker. The constable says she was buried inside the marshland. When I asked him why she was cast so far from her townsmen, he told me that it was Starkcrowe's will. The pastor wished to show his contempt for the spiritually weak. I feel terrible putting that to paper, but I know you appreciate honesty. Starkcrowe wanted to make an example of a suicide. Your mother is that example.

I will write again soon, hopefully with news of your sister. I still have hope that she will appear. Kiss our baby as I cannot, and think of me fondly.

Your husband,
Joseph

7

"You're sure you're ready to go?" Mom hovered as I swept through my room packing a duffel bag.

No.

"Yes," I said as brightly as I could. "It's a summer vacation! It'll be fine."

She stood in the doorway in a belted-off purple robe, her hair in a clip, her bare toes peeking out from below the hem. Every time I looked at her, she looked away. We were both embarrassed, but I had too much on my mind to sweat her personal life right now.

Like Mary coming at us from the coffee table. Like Joseph Simpson's letter to Constance. He said he had more questions than answers. I did, too, now that I knew Starkcrowe married Elizabeth Hawthorne. It was too convenient.

I wonder if they worked together to kill Mary.

"What are you planning to do while you're there?" Mom asked.

"The usual. Bonfires, canoeing. Summer stuff."

That's how it used to be, Mom. Before I knew how scary The Folly was. How did I not notice it for all those summers?

I brushed past her to collect my toiletries from the bathroom.

She followed. "And Kitty will be with you the whole time?"

"Yes."

"Jess's parents are fine with this?" Mom stayed on my heels, closer than my shadow.

"Yes," I lied. "It's only a week, Mom. Enjoy yourself while I'm gone." Mom had her hand over her eyes, the tips of her ears blazing red. "Spend some time with your friend. He makes you happy?"

Mom peered at me through splayed fingers. "Yes, but not at your expense."

"My expense what? I made it through my junior year. I'm alive."

Barely. Barely alive. I came so close, Mom. You have no idea.

I zipped my bag closed.

"Are you and Jess still fighting?" she pressed.

"No."

Mom frowned as I hauled my stuff to the living room. I looked out the windows and down at the parking lot, waiting for Kitty. The glass was all new, the panes replaced after Mary grabbed Bronx and splattered him across the pavement.

Two surgeries to fix him so far, at least one more to go.

Mom hovered behind me. "I know I'm being clingy, but after everything that's happened..." She shuffled across the carpet and then her arms were around me, squeezing me in a fierce bear hug from behind. "I don't feel good about this. I'm not going to stop you, but I'll miss you. Text me every night?"

"I promise. Every night." I threaded my fingers with Mom's and leaned back against her, my head settling in the crook of her neck. "I will. I love you, Mom."

⁂

Kitty had on the blackest sunglasses I'd ever seen. She insisted she wasn't hungover, but by the green hue to her skin and the way her lips puckered whenever I sipped my coffee, I didn't believe her.

I rotated my phone to look at Jess's e-mail. I'd read it aloud to Kitty twice already, but she hadn't said much about it yet.

"Are you okay?" I asked.

"No. Mary grabbed me again. I have PTSD going on," she snapped.

I stopped examining the letter to blink at her profile. Crinkled brow, pinched lips, flared nostrils. She was angry. "Sorry. I didn't mean, like—I know that. Sorry."

Kitty's cheeks ballooned before she exhaled a steady stream of air. "I'm sorry. I feel like crap and I'm jumping at shadows. I can see the reflection of my eyes in my sunglasses and it's bugging me out."

"Been there, done that. It's no fun, but at least we're together," I said. "Do you want me to take the glasses?"

Kitty shook her head. "The sun is killing me. Headache."

No hangover, my ass.

The GPS beeped on Kitty's dashboard when we reached Cody's street. Kitty eased onto the curb across from a gray house with dingy white trim. Some improvements had been made since our last visit. The lawn had been mowed. The windows were clear, and all of the buckets Cody had used to transport pigs' blood were washed and stacked in a pile. Boards covered the hole in the front step, and the rusted-out Volkswagen was gone from the driveway.

The front door of the screened-in porch swung open. Cody emerged holding two Home Depot bags. She was still as pale as paper, her scars slick and pink and crisscrossing her face like a hash mark. Her dark hair had been cut short, in a boy cut, the sides and top sprinkled with gray. She wasn't old—in her thirties—but the years with Mary had aged her.

Cody stopped at the end of the driveway. "I'm ready. We should go to the church now, when the light is best," she said. Her good eye skimmed my face before jumping to Kitty. "You'll drive."

It wasn't a question.

Kitty stared. "Yeah, sure. Hi, nice to meet you."

"Hi. I'm Cody. You're Kitty." Cody opened the back of the car and threw in the bags.

"How are y—"

"Do you need directions to the church?" Cody interjected in her low, raspy voice. Kitty looked as if she didn't know if she should laugh or be offended. She had seen Cody only for a moment the last time we came out to The Folly, when Cody was a wreck. Cody was better groomed now, with new jeans, a new T-shirt, and a black patch on her face, but her demeanor was as unpolished as ever.

"Yes, please," Kitty replied. "I wasn't with everyone else the last time."

Cody climbed into the backseat and buckled up. She looked at the windows surrounding her and appeared to melt into her seat, keeping her body low and hunched like a squatting troll. "Get back on the highway, take the next exit. I have salt, lanterns, sledgehammers, shovels, and buckets for the water. Muck boots, too, so we won't have to deal with bat shit."

As Kitty guided us out of the quiet neighborhood, I handed my cell phone to Cody. She looked confused, but seeing the letter from Joseph, she started reading. Before long, she was shaking the phone. "How do I see the rest of it?"

I gawked at her for not knowing, but then I remembered she'd been inside of that house for seventeen years. Smartphones weren't a thing when she went into reclusion. She'd never e-mailed me or talked about a computer, because she'd been totally cut off from the outside world.

"Like this," I said, taking the phone and swiping my thumb across the screen. She scowled and took the phone back to read the rest of the letter.

"Interesting," she said. A passing car flashed in the window beside her and she yelped, pancaking herself to the seat. Her hands slapped at her pockets until she found a Ziploc bag full of salt. She opened it and palmed some granules, eyeballing the glass beside her and twitching.

I did a sweep of the car looking for phantom faces. "It's okay. She's not here. We're safe."

Cody hid her face into her shoulder, her eyes cast to the car floor.

Kitty got us back on the highway, or what counted as a high-way in Solomon's Folly—one lane in each direction, thick trees to either side of the road, and beyond that, green stretches of undeveloped land. I could see cows in the distance, a smear of gray clouds threatening to cloak the summer sky, and a deep valley dotted with small lakes and brush.

Cody skimmed a hand down her face as if she could replace her scared face with a more assured one. "That's the swamp from the letter. The Hockomock swamp. You've heard of it?"

"I don't know much about it," I admitted. We sometimes drove past it on the way to the grocery store. At night, the fog roiled from its depths, oozing across the road and blanketing everything in eerie white. "I know it's big and wet and there was a war between the Native Americans and the settlers there a long time ago. King Philip's War."

Kitty nodded. "My dad hunts there. Or hunted, a long time ago. He says it's gross. Like, thick and hard to get around in."

Cody snorted. "He's right. It's also haunted, which should make looking for Hannah Worth's gravesite interesting. That's the plan, after the church."

The idea of a haunted swamp cramped my brain. It wasn't

that I didn't believe it so much as I didn't *want* to believe it. Ghosts drifting through the marshlands? Monsters howling at the moon? What was next—aliens and Sasquatch?

Cody caught my incredulous expression in the window and shook her head. "How is *that* ridiculous and Mary isn't?"

"It's not," I admitted. "I just don't know what to do about it."

"There's nothing you *can* do about it." Cody leaned forward to point at an approaching exit. Her nails were bitten down so far, they'd bled. Rust smeared the peachy fingertips. "We're sticking to the plan. Look for Mary's body, then find Hannah. I don't want to go into the swamp. No one wants to go into the swamp if they have half a brain, but we have to. I have to." Cody paused and looked out the window. "Moira was brave enough. My cousin. She had this idea that the swamp was why Mary rose. The curse on the land."

"What do you mean by cursed land?" Kitty asked, steering the car off the main drag.

"The swamp is bloody. Thirty-six hundred people died in or near it during King Philip's War, a lot of them Native Americans. People say the spirits of the dead linger there, which is why Solomon Hawthorne was able to settle there. No one else wanted it."

"Wait, the town's founding father was related to Elizabeth Hawthorne?"

Cody nodded. "The Hawthornes are all over The Folly, and most of them are assholes, like their ancestor. Solomon emigrated from England over three hundred years ago. First thing he did was seduce a girl already engaged to someone else. The Puritans kicked him out, so he struck out on his own. There wasn't as much unclaimed land left as he'd hoped, so he ended up building in the swamp. He's lucky he survived. The Hockomock is dangerous. Wild dogs—coyotes bred with domesticated dogs that rove in packs. Quicksand the locals call Black Betty. Undergrowth, overgrowth. Somehow, Solomon's Falls rose to prosperity anyway. The question is how?"

"You mean Solomon's Folly," I corrected.

"No, I mean Falls. It didn't become Folly until half of the town was butchered twenty years after it was founded. Hockomock means 'where spirits dwell' in Wampanoag. Considering how many people have died here over the years? Considering *Mary*? It's appropriate."

8

Daylight did little to strip the church of its ominous veneer. Gray stone blackened by time, mildew growing in the cracks and stretching toward a half-collapsed roof. The steeple was gone, but I could see the crumbling remnants of it at the back of the property. The side was collapsed as if it'd been punched in by a giant. A cracked bell lay on its side amidst the rubble, the loop at the top disintegrated to rust.

There were no front doors, so we could see directly into the church's empty belly. Broken stone littered the floor. A moldy bureau was pressed against the far wall, though how it got there I didn't know. We'd pushed it aside last visit. The door that kept Mary Worth locked in darkness was behind that bureau.

Someone's been here since our last visit.

Someone looking for Mary?

Jess?

The windows along the south side of the church had no glass.

A tree poked through the time-ravaged frames, new buds clinging to the branch tips. Twin archways opened up into side rooms
that we hadn't explored.

Cody boldly entered the church. Kitty eased along behind
her, her hand skimming the walls. Her head swiveled like a cat
exploring a house for the first time. No matter how hard I willed
myself to follow them, I couldn't make my feet go.

*Mary lunging up from the cold water. My body smashing
against the stone steps. Mary's fist, slimy and fishlike, clenching
in my hair, pulling my head back. My screams echoing through
the basement as Mary tried to drown me in a pool of water.
Blackness in my vision. Water in my nose. Water in my ears,
muffling my friends' terrified shrieks.*

"Shauna?"

Kitty turned back and offered her hand. I stared at it, swallowing hard. Five feet felt like five hundred, but when I couldn't
go to Kitty, Kitty came to me, pressing our palms together, tugging me through the doorway.

Side by side, we walked into the church. It had been wet last
time, the stones slick and covered with bat refuse. Now it was
drier, everything baked to caked mud from the sun.

Cody tromped from the left room to the right. She never
looked at us, her Home Depot bags clunking at her sides. "Nothing except broken lumber in the last one. Stones in this one from
the collapsed side wall. Let's head down."

We pushed the bureau aside until there was only the old
wooden door with its rusted lock between us and the basement.
Cody dropped one of the bags so she could fiddle with it. I heard

the click, the grinding of the gears of the lock, and the squeal as she forced it ajar. I ducked, expecting a bat stampede. The air was still.

Cody donned our single pair of boots. She pulled out a series of lanterns and eased down the narrow stairs, placing a light every three steps. I stayed up top, my arms crossed over my chest. Kitty hesitated, but then followed Cody, handing her whatever she needed from the orange bags.

I glanced at the ceiling, expecting to see the beady, onyx eyes of a thousand mini-predators, but it was flat stone and mildew. I'd read that spirits perfumed their haunts with a certain type of energy. Happier spirits could make the air warm and smell like flowers. But we'd woken Mary down here. Her rising poisoned the atmosphere, too much for even the bats. And, it seemed, too much for the beetles; there'd been a small-scale epidemic of pincher bugs the last time, but I hadn't spotted a single one so far.

"Buckets," Cody said. "We need to drain the puddle so we can look at the floor." What followed was an assembly line, with Cody scooping buckets of water, handing them to Kitty, and Kitty handing them to me. I splashed them over the stone floor of the church, watching the water settle into the cracks between the stones.

It took a while to get anywhere. I kept thinking Cody would call up to tell us she could see stone, but then Kitty would hand me more water. After what felt like forever, Cody crouched to examine the floor.

"Gloves. I think we're finished."

I pawed through the supply bag to hand down gloves and a three-pronged hoe. Cody started to dig, shoving broken bricks, pebbles, and grit aside as she prodded the dip in the floor.

I moved farther into the basement, down three more steps so I could watch. Without the water, the divot became more defined. Seven feet long, three feet wide, and a foot deep at its lowest point. Cody squatted at the corner of it, still working on removing the topmost pieces of stone. The crusty layer slowly peeled away, revealing thick, sodden mud.

"Hand me the sifter," she said.

It was the last thing in the bag. Cody loaded it with mud and shook it out, letting big droplets of gook splash down on the stones outside the crater. She panned, like a miner looking for gold, but uncovered nothing. She took the hoe to the ground, clawing through the earth with so much ferocity, she spattered her face and Kitty's jeans.

Kitty and I couldn't do much to help, so we waited in silence.

Cody abandoned the hoe to work with her hands, her fingers raking through the muck. "I see something. Bring another lantern down."

The mud squished and burped as Cody dug through it. Brown-black smears stained her from fingertips to wrists, the sludge climbing toward the opening of the gloves near her elbows. She scooped handful after handful, throwing the mess at the stacked crates against the opposite wall from the stairs.

Cody continued working. I leaned forward to watch, but then I heard a sound from behind. My head jerked around, eyes narrowing as I peered out up the stairs.

Tap, screeeee.

Tap, screeeee.

Tap, screeeee.

It was rhythmic and getting louder.

Getting *closer.*

"Guys. Do you hear that?"

Mary heaving herself from the basement's depths, limbs bent at odd angles as she skittered onto the church floor. The strange animal chitters as she gave chase. The rat-a-tat of palms and feet striking stone as she rushed us, moving more like a spider than a human.

Kitty lifted her head. "Hear what?"

"Don't move the lantern," Cody snapped. "I see gold!"

"Sorry!" Kitty leaned forward to cast better light on Cody's dig.

Tap, screeeee.

Tap, screeeee.

I reached into my pocket for the salt, my thumb popping the top off the mint container, just as Cody let out a whoop behind me.

"Look at this!"

I wanted to, but a figure had appeared at the top of the stairs. Tall, slender. The way the sun hit, I couldn't make out features, but by its approach—her approach—I knew it wasn't Mary. Unless Mary had gotten herself a cane, a purple track suit, and a shock of short, silver hair.

"This is private property," the stranger said in greeting. "Though I'm guessing you're Jessica's friends."

The woman moved into proper light and I got my first good look at her. Deep lines around her eyes and mouth, putting her well into her seventies. Blue eyes, a narrow nose, a wide mouth, and only one ear. There was a hole on the left side of her head instead of cartilage.

"Aunt Dell?" I'd seen pictures of the woman in her younger years, but I hadn't noticed her disfigurement before.

"You must be Shauna. Yes, hello. I'm Jessica's aunt." She shuffled my way, one foot stepping like normal, the other lagging behind. The noise I'd heard was her walking stick striking rock followed by the drag of her leg.

She stopped at the top of the stairs, peering down at me and the other girls. Pinched between two of Cody's fingers, roundish and dull gold beneath smears of thick mud, was what appeared to be a locket embossed with an ornate *W*.

9

I looked from the locket to the others surrounding me. Everyone had a claim to the treasure—Cody and me because of our hauntings, Kitty because of Anna, Dell because of her blood tie to Mary—but Cody wasn't relinquishing it. I desperately wanted to snatch it from her fist to examine it, but I was pretty sure Cody would have fought me. Considering the trowel in her other hand, she would have won.

She pulled the locket to her chest to stake her claim. Kitty and I wouldn't challenge her, but Dell was another story. We were on her private property trespassing for a second time in so many months. If any of us had the right to demand Cody hand it over, it was the woman who held the deed to the land.

Instead, Dell's hands clasped the pommel of her walking stick. "If you want answers about Mary Worth, I can help," she said. "Will you join me for tea?"

Cody looked from the dip in the floor to the necklace. "We're not done here. And we were going to try to find Hannah Worth's grave today, too. We need daylight for that."

Dell nodded. "I can help with that, too. Please, come with me."

Cody twitched and muttered to herself, distressed. I understood; Jess couldn't be trusted. Why should we assume her aunt was any better?

"Fine. If it's quick," she relented.

Dell smirked and tapped her cane on the floor. "It's as quick as you choose to make it, Miss Jackson." Aunt Dell knew who we all were, it seemed.

Cody pocketed the necklace and gathered her digging tools. Kitty snuffed the lanterns. Dell hobbled outside and stood off to the side to stay out of everyone's way. I went with her, relieved to be out of that basement. Too many bad memories lived in the shadows. The trapped, musty smell turned my stomach.

Cody and Kitty followed, sludgy mud trailing behind Cody's boots. The Home Depot bags clunked at Kitty's sides.

Dell motioned at the river with her cane. "Wash the boots so they won't soil the interior of your car."

I waited for Cody to take off the boots and brought them to the riverbank, careful not to get too close to the steeper mud. Within seconds of plunging my hands into the water, my fingertips went numb, the joints in my knuckles aching. It was freezing. I sloughed off the mud as fast as I could, gritting my teeth against the stabbing cold.

Poor Hannah Worth, drowning in such a frigid place.

A hard rush of water nearly tore the boots from my grasp.

I scrambled away from the river, the boots clasped to my chest and raining cold water down the front of my T-shirt.

"I can drive you home if you'd like," I heard Kitty say to Dell. I threw the boots in the back of the SUV alongside the Home Depot bags.

"It's a short walk. Your car is safe here." Cody, Kitty, and I shared a look before falling into step behind Jess's aunt, rats to her Pied Piper.

We walked parallel to the river until we came to a small bridge. Three arced coves let water run through, the walls constructed of stone and packed cement. Posts at either end allowed people and bikes to pass over, but no cars. A faded orange sign read UNDER CONSTRUCTION, but it was evident no one had serviced the bridge in a long time.

Dell paused halfway across, pointing up the river at an exaggerated bend. "The constable's men claimed they found Hannah's body in that elbow. The report mentions the bridge being not far south from the corpse and tucked inside a bend. It's the only one on this stretch of the river."

"Did she really kill herself?" Kitty asked.

"No." Dell's curt reply didn't invite further questions.

We walked. Dell's house was an old New England farmhouse with white shingles and black shutters. The fence had seen better days; there were as many planks on the ground as there were connecting the posts. A shed that looked suspiciously like an outhouse occupied the left side of the lawn. A barn converted into a garage took up the right. The tree in the front yard was spindly and dry, its bark gone black, the branches barren.

The inside was cluttered with furniture. It was also dusty; silver picture frames were dulled to gray from a thick layer of grime. Black soot smudged the walls above where Dell burned candles, and the corners of the room dripped with lacy cobwebs. It still managed to be homey, though—overstuffed mauve couches in front of the fireplace, crocheted blankets folded in neat stacks, and shelves upon shelves of knickknacks.

Dell motioned us toward the living room, her cane waving at a fat orange cat with long hair. "Make yourselves at home while I steep the tea. Don't mind Horace. He runs the place."

Kitty ran her hand along Horace's spine while I wandered toward Dell's curio cabinet. Family photos sat propped along the back, surrounded by ceramic cats and angel statues.

"It smells like dead flowers in here," Cody griped.

"Potpourri," Kitty said. "On the coffee table."

Cody grunted and settled into the chair by the fireplace, her head tilting back to examine the portraits on the walls. The necklace chain looped around her knuckles, the links caked with dirt. Her thumb swept over the dented gold case, a ragged thumbnail prying dried mud from the creases.

Jess's smiling face loomed from the mantel. Her junior year yearbook photo. She looked fresh-faced and pretty, with her flawless complexion and long, flowing hair. Not at all like the scarred, terrified girl I'd seen at a party the night before.

"Notice there's no glass," Cody said in a low voice.

She gestured at a painting of a cottage in a field of pastel flowers. "No glass in any of the frames." My eyes jumped from picture to picture. No glass protection.

"That's because Mary appears in reflections, of course," Aunt Dell said, pushing a wheeled cart into the room. There was a china set with a steaming pot, delicate ivory teacups, and a platter of jammy cookies.

Kitty glanced up from the cat. "You worry about Mary?"

"Every Worth girl does. We'd be crazy not to. Help your-selves." Dell poured herself a cup of tea. The process of adding a sugar cube, a dash of milk, and two cookies to her saucer looked like a long-practiced routine. She settled into one of the chairs, peering at all of us over the rim of her teacup. Her eyes were cornflower blue. Jess's shade. It was disconcerting.

"But your niece was the one who summoned her. If you all know about her, why would she do that?" Cody demanded. She opened her hand and the necklace dropped, dangling from her fingertips. Dell leaned forward in her chair to take a closer look.

"Did you want to wash that? The bathroom is down the hall to the right," Dell said, pointing behind her.

Cody shook her head. "I will, but first, tell me—us—why the Worth girls fear Mary."

Dell returned her teacup to the saucer, the china clink-ing. She lifted a cookie and examined it, as if it had somehow become more interesting than her guests. "Let me ask you and Shauna something." Dell glanced up. The lines on her face were so deeply etched into her skin, she looked like a leather purse. "When Mary appeared, did you hurt her? Ever do her any harm?"

Cody answered before I could. "I slashed her arms with knives. I went through her hand with a butcher's knife once.

I struck her with mallets and hammers, but she always came back."

Dell nodded but continued to peer at me. I wanted to answer, but the words wouldn't come. My tongue was a slab of granite in my mouth.

Kitty's basement, Mary holding Jess hostage. Screams. So many screams—Kitty and Jess both more terrified than I had ever seen. Kitty throwing salt, the room littered with broken bottles and shattered furniture. Jamming the broken stool leg into Mary's face. Connecting with the eye socket. Mary's flesh yielding, like moldy pudding stuck to bone.

"Shauna took out her eye," Kitty said. "With a stick."

Dell nibbled the cookie, her head tilted in thought. Her hair shifted, letting me see the ear hole without the attached ear. I tried not to stare, but it looked so strange, like her head was off-balance. Was she was born that way or...

"She took it," Dell said.

Heat flooded my cheeks. I could hear my mother's voice in my head, chastising me for being rude. "Sorry. I—yeah. Sorry. I didn't mean to...you know."

"Quite fine." Dell lifted the hair and turned her head so all of us could see, though Kitty couldn't bring herself to look. "Mary took it thirty years ago." Dell let the hair drop, using the half-eaten cookie to gesture around the room. "She needs to fix herself, you see. It's not really magic. It's more"—Dell paused as she searched for the proper word—"harvesting."

"Harvesting," Cody repeated. "Like..."

"Oh, God." I wished I didn't understand what Dell meant,

but I did. The previous night, Mary's arm was rotten and gray except for one tiny sliver of pink. A finger. A finger that looked at odds with the rest of the steel-blue parts.

A *new* finger.

"Anna," I whispered.

⤫

Kitty's sobs filled the room. She puffed on her inhaler before collapsing into a pile of misery beside me. I stroked her hair and waited out the storm.

Cody hunched in her chair, her dirty fingertips stroking the satin of her eye patch every few minutes. She'd lost the eye to Mary some years back. She'd never mentioned Mary recycling parts because I was pretty sure it never occurred to her. To find out she'd become part of the very monster she loathed ... I couldn't imagine it. Mary had cut me, but she'd never taken a part of me and made it her own.

"I saw a pink finger last night," I said quietly. "It looked out of place on her hand. Are you saying that belonged to Anna?" I reached over to squeeze Kitty's knee in reassurance.

"No. Your friend died a month ago," Dell said, "If it's pink, it's fresh. The replacement parts deteriorate like any dead flesh. Mary must have bled someone new. Not Jessica. I spoke with her this morning. But if there's a new part and Jessica's tag remains—" Dell cleared her throat. "Someone got pulled into the mirror, God help them."

I ran my hands down my face.

Another missing girl on the five o'clock news.

"So what does that mean?!" Cody rasped. Her body twitched every few seconds, the fury too much for her to contain. "You said the Worth girls fear Mary. When are you going to explain?"

Dell's look wasn't friendly. "I was getting there, Miss Jackson. Don't rush me."

Cody clutched the armrests of her chair as if they were necks she wanted to strangle. The necklace dangled from her fingers to sweep the floor. Dell's cat readied to pounce, but Cody jerked it back and pocketed it before Horace could attack.

"I've waited a long time for some answers," Cody spat.

Dell retrieved her tea, sipping daintily with her pinky raised. She took her time replacing the cup onto the saucer, her expression guarded. "Mary haunts those she bleeds but can't pull into the mirror. She obsesses, tracking them by the scent of their blood. It calls to her and sustains her. But sometimes no one summons for a long time and her body deteriorates. She's ghostly, yes, but she's something more, too. Ghoulish. She preserves her physical form by recycling parts from her victims."

Dell wasn't looking directly at any of us. "If Mary doesn't get fresh stock, she finds what she knows, and what she knows is her own blood. Worth girl blood. Jessica summoned the ghost so she didn't succumb the way my aunt did in the sixties. The way I almost did a decade later."

I stared at the old woman trying so damned hard to not look any of us in the eye.

"Your aunt died to Mary?"

For a fleeting moment, Dell looked sad. "Yes. Like so many others, which is why Jess summoned Mary. She wants to end the family curse. Our family has been dying to Mary Worth for almost as long as she's been dead."

❧

It took a half hour, an Ativan, and a call to Bronx to relax Kitty. She sprawled across Dell's couch, body cocooned in an afghan, Horace the cat perched on her hip. Her eyes were half-mast and swollen, her nose Rudolph red. I could hear the rush of water as Cody rinsed the necklace in the bathroom. Dell swept through the house, collecting manila envelopes, photo albums, and notebooks. She dropped them on the coffee table beside the serving cart.

"Why now?" Kitty asked from the couch, sounding sleepy and content. It was a chemically induced calm, but I was envious of it all the same. "Did Jess just find out about Mary?"

Dell settled into her seat, her joints sounding like dry sticks snapping. "I'm old and tired. Without me, Mary falls to Jessica. I had to warn her. She took it better than I expected. She wanted to make Mary move on to the afterlife, so she'd stop hurting people. I believe that's her ultimate goal, but she's taken grave risks in her pursuit."

"Anna was that risk," I said quietly. "She tried to sacrifice Kitty, too."

Dell swept the back of her hand across her brow like the revelation made her faint. "She was scared and wrong. I'm sorry. I don't really know what I can say."

Silently, Kitty reached for the tea cart to fix herself a cup, but I did it for her. Kitty had been fierce since Anna's death, but there was a frailty there, too. Maybe I was like Aunt Dell— fruitlessly apologizing with tea and shoulder rubs because I hadn't had the foresight to stop Jess when I had the chance.

Dell looked at the pile of envelopes, pictures, and binders. "I don't know where to start." She bent forward, grunting as she produced a black-and-white photograph of a woman dressed in an old-fashioned nurse's uniform. By the curled style of her blond hair and the way she'd painted her lips dark, I guessed the picture was from the thirties or forties. "This is my aunt, Prudence. She was the Worth afflicted before me, and the one who accidentally unleashed Mary on the world at large in the sixties. Instead of waiting for Mary to find her in the glass, Pru gathered her friends and called for her. She was impatient, like Jessica. And me, I suppose. Impatience is a Worth woman failing. Anyway, it didn't work the first time, but the second. Well. Mary claimed her first free-world victim—Pru's friend Gerdy."

"What changed between the first and second summoning?" I asked.

"Pru figured out that imploring Mary to come didn't work, so they mocked her, like the girls had mocked her in the basement years ago. That got Mary's attention."

Dell punctuated it by producing a copy of a letter I'd already seen. It was Mary's last, the one she wrote to her sister explaining how Elizabeth Hawthorne and her friends had teased her through the basement door.

Dell's fingertip grazed the last lines.

Bloody Mary. Bloody Mary. Bloody Mary.

"We're taunting her like her bullies taunted her," I whispered. It was awful in a way, almost like we deserved—

No. No one deserved Mary. But there was an undeniable cruelty to the summons.

The water stopped running and Cody reemerged, the clean necklace lying flat across her palm. "Look what I have," she said, wagging it back and forth. The locket gleamed despite its long years buried beneath the church floor. "The picture inside is completely rotted, but the gold is intact."

Dell stirred behind me. She removed photographs from the albums, some of the pictures so old they were printed on wooden plates instead of film paper. She gestured at the curio behind her.

"Second drawer, Shauna. Get my magnifying glass? We're on a necklace hunt. I don't want to assume this is Mary's locket without some evidence."

I quickly found the magnifying glass in a nest of colored yarn and knitting needles.

"Thank you."

"You have so much stuff," Kitty said in wonderment. "Family stuff. We have some old pictures, but this is something else."

Dell squinted at her first picture, using the glass to examine the finer details. "I'm a steward of sorts, Miss Kitty. I was the one saddled with Mary, like my aunt was before me. None of my relatives have been able to put Mary to rest, so we care for these relics in hopes that the next generation will figure out what we didn't. Constance lived her whole life trying to help her sister but was never successful. The only thing she could do was preserve Mary's things in hopes that something would eventually change."

Dell tilted her picture this way and that before handing it to me. It was an image of a younger Mary, before all the tragedy, wearing a dark dress and holding the Bible to her chest. Her hair hung long and straight to her waist. Beside her was an older girl with blond hair pinned to her head. Constance.

The sisters looked so happy with their faint smiles and bright eyes.

Cody sidled up to the coffee table, sitting cross-legged on the floor as she sorted the pile, not only the photographs but notes and letters, too. Kitty scooted over on the couch to help, all of us falling into library silence, passing noteworthy discoveries back and forth.

It didn't take long to go through the photographs. I held up a picture of Mary standing with a group of girls her age, perhaps fourteen or fifteen. I recognized Elizabeth Hawthorne immediately. She brooded at the camera, whereas Mary was, once again, smiling. The girls were bundled in their winter coats; snow frosted the ground and shrubs to either side of them. The collar of Mary's dark overcoat was parted enough that I could see a hint of something at her neck. I'd seen her wear a cross before, but that necklace wasn't the right shape.

"Aunt Dell, look at this?" I offered Dell the picture so she could examine it with her magnifying glass. As I stretched across the table, Cody snatched for me, her cold fingers almost cutting off the circulation in my wrist. I yelped, more surprised than hurt, but Cody waved a photocopy of a letter under my nose.

"Read this," she demanded. "Now."

Joseph,

I'm writing to tell you my sister is dead. She did not run
away as some have claimed. I know this as I know the sun will
rise. There's been no news from the local authorities. No one from
The Folly has contacted me. No, I've seen Mary's ghost with my
own eyes. She's dead and gone and haunting me in any surface
that reflects light. I implore you to read on before assuming that
I'm mad.

I was rocking Edward to sleep when I first saw the face.
It looked like someone standing outside of the house windows
looking in. It was pale faced and small framed, and at first I
thought it was a child.

I have done as you instructed—the doors are locked in your
absence, and the new groundskeeper, Mr. Hallingsway, is always
beside me. After seeing the stranger, I asked him to look around
the property. He took the dogs on a tour but found nothing. What
was curious, however, was that the dogs refused to enter the
house. They stopped in the doorway, snarling. Mr. Hallingsway
walked the halls to ensure no one had forced their way in, but the
house was empty.

Two days passed before I saw the face again. I had just
bathed. Edward was with your mother and sisters at a picnic
in the park. I dressed myself in our room. As I passed the vanity
mirror, I saw the face peering out at me. This time, there was a

hand pressed against the glass as if pushing out from the inside. Spectral mists cloaked much of my vision. I screamed for the staff, but the figure vanished as soon as Miss Winchester dashed into the room.

This happened a half-dozen times over the next few days. Each time the stranger hid from me. The only constant was the hand upon the glass. I thought it a ghostly trick, but then I noticed that the pads of the fingers were flattened. It really did appear that someone was trapped on the other side.

Details became easier to discern thereafter. The body deteriorated between visits, going from peach and pink to shades of gray, green, and blue. The veins turned black, and the flesh cracked open. There were insects, too! Black water beetles that crawled all over. It made my skin itch to see them.

I didn't believe at first that it was my sister. Perhaps that was stupid, but hope is all I've had to cling to since your departure. Last evening I was forced to reconcile what in my heart I think I already knew. I rocked Edward in his nursery, humming a song my mother used to sing to Mary when she was a baby. Edward slept upon my breast. I stood to put him in his cradle when I spied the figure in the window, peering in. The fingers pressed to the glass, streaking down the pane as if pawing. Again there was a strange, swirling mist blocking my view.

Every previous visit, I'd run from the room, fearful of the phantom. Last night, I held Edward to my heart and waited. This must have been what the ghost wanted, as the fog cleared and I beheld my sister's face. I wept. It's bloated in some parts, saggy in others, and her eyes are sunken and black. She wears a white dress that drips with water. Her hair is tangled and matted with leaves and mud.

Part of me wanted to flee, but I forced myself to stay. Mary lingered, too, her hand stroking the windowpane. Tears streamed down my cheeks as I approached. She didn't speak. I lifted my hand to hers, expecting only cold glass between us, but I swear on our son that she reached through the window and clasped my hand, her fingers locking with mine. Dead flesh, Joseph.

She released me and faded into the glass. I have not yet seen her today.

You'll want to come home upon receiving this letter, I know, but I beg you to continue your business in Boston. The trial is so close to conclusion. Perhaps when you are done we can revisit Solomon's Folly and search for Mary and Mother's remains together? The baby is old enough to stay with your mother awhile I would think. It would soothe my soul to know I put this uneasy spirit to rest.

Thinking of you always and forever, beloved.

Constance

10

"He never found Mary that first visit," I said more to myself than anyone else. "That's so sad." Kitty took the letter, skimming the lines. She tapped the upper corner of the page, thinking. "Mary didn't appear for six months after her death? Why? And why can she see Mary if she's a mother?"

"I don't know for certain," Dell said. "And Mary is willing to make exceptions for Worth girls regarding the mothers. The blood calls to her too strongly."

She handed me the picture and the magnifying glass so I could look. Only half of the necklace was visible beneath Mary's collar, but it was the same ovular shape, the same relative size with an initial. A match. Cody quickly snatched the photo from my fingers.

Dell continued. "The necklace means one of two things. One, that it fell off while Mary was down in that basement and it somehow got covered lat—"

"No," Cody interrupted. "I had to dig. It was a foot and a half down, maybe two. If it'd been kicked under the rocks, it wouldn't have been so deep."

Dell cast me a look, an eyebrow raised as if I was supposed to explain Cody's demeanor, but I wasn't telling a woman twice my age to be polite. It wasn't my place.

Dell glanced down at the jacket of her tracksuit, plucking lint from the velvet. "Well, there you have it. There is no option two according to Miss Jackson."

"That letter is unbelievably creepy." Kitty reached out to haul Horace up onto her chest, her fingers trailing along his spine. "At least Mary didn't attack Constance."

"No. Mary still had some sense of herself then. It worsened over time." Dell's eyes strayed to the wall clock, an old-fashioned Felix the Cat affair with ticktock eyes. "It's two. If we want to look for Hannah, we should leave now. She's along the outer edges of the swamp, toward Samoset's Perch, I believe. That's not a place you go at night. I hope you all have sneakers. Shauna, Kitty—take the pictures with you if you want. You can look at them tonight as long as you promise to return them in the same condition you received them."

That seemed like a good idea. I doubted there was much we'd find that Dell hadn't already, but my experience with Jess taught me it was better to do the research myself, not count on others being forthright with information.

"Wait, you *believe?*" Cody said. "How are we going to find Hannah if you don't know for sure? We should know where we're going. The Hockomock is a hellhole." Cody licked her lips and twitched. Her hand smacked down at her arm as if she was smushing a bug no one else could see.

"I have a good idea of where we're going. I've been out looking before. Joseph left some notes that were helpful."

Cody and Dell shared a long, intense stare that made my skin itch. I organized the pictures and papers, half so Dell didn't come home to a mess, half so I didn't have to get involved in the escalating tension. Kitty joined my tidying efforts without a word.

Cody's uncomfortable. She doesn't trust Dell. She knows something I don't.

I'd just gotten the last note tucked into the accordion folder when I heard tires on gravel followed by a car door slamming. Kitty tensed beside me. Cody went to the front windows and thrust the curtain aside to get a clear look at the driveway.

"Hell," she spat.

I glanced up. "What?"

"Jess."

Feet pounding, the wail of oil-starved door hinges, and deep, heavy breaths. Kitty reached for me, digging her fingernails into my forearm. Her eyes bulged from their sockets. *We need to get out of here*, her expression said. I'd just offered my hand in a show of solidarity when Jess careened into sight.

The blood was everywhere.

It oozed from the side of her head, matting her hair to her scalp and dribbling in rivers down her cheeks and neck. The ragged tatters of her shirt hugged her body, the fabric so saturated it was stiff in parts. I could see gouges in her sides, the slashes parallel like a claw rake. Her eye was puffy and black, her nostril crusted with rust. Purple bruises covered her face, her chest, her arms. She smelled like blood—that coppery tang that reminded me of pennies or steak that had been on the counter too long.

Fear ricocheted through my body. My legs were so weak, it felt like my bones had melted. This hadn't been a minor scuffle. Mary had *pulverized* Jess.

"Oh, Jessica. Oh, no." Dell's voice was whisper soft. Her hand flew up to cover her mouth and she stared, as shaken by the sight of Jess as the rest of us.

Jess didn't answer. I wasn't sure she could. Dell maneuvered her into a chair, tutting and fussing the entire time. Her hands slid through the gore, but she didn't hesitate. She touched Jess on the head, on the neck, examining her wounds with bloody fingers. "Did you drive here from Bridgewater? How? Good God. Someone get me a towel. Talk to me, Jessica."

Kitty and I were too stunned to move. Cody shook it off first; she dashed for the bathroom to get towels and hot water. Kitty broke away from me to go to Jess's side. She used Kleenex to dash at Jess's bloody cheek. Even after everything Jess put us through, Kitty was quick to help.

"She's out," Jess mumbled. Her fingers lifted to her mouth, prodding at her fat, rubbery lips. They looked twice as big as usual. "Mary's out. She came for me and chased me and she's out now."

"Shhh. Sit still while I look at you," Dell said. Cody rushed in with the towels, and Dell began cleaning the head injury, meticulously moving Jess's hair around so she could better see the extent of the damage.

"No, you don't understand. She's not trapped in the glass anymore. She's out. I broke the mirror she passed through. When she didn't disappear, I locked her in the basement and drove here. She's out. I freed her by accident."

I didn't understand. I looked to Dell, hoping for insight, but she'd gone still, the towel poised above Jess's scalp. "What do you mean you broke the glass?" Dell asked, voice so soft I almost didn't hear it.

Jess whimpered. "She came from the sliding porch doors. I'd just gotten home..." Jess stammered, fumbling her words before letting loose with a sob. Jess wasn't a crier; when she broke her ankle during junior high softball sliding into home plate, she'd never shed a tear, but this was different. She slumped in her seat, blood gushing onto the mauve upholstery.

"She chased me, and I managed to get her into the basement. I locked it. I thought if I broke the doors she came from she'd go away forever. I hardened the glass with salt and then smashed it with a chair. But she was still there. She didn't find another mirror. She stayed. So I ran. She must have broken the door down. I watched her chase my car in the rearview mirror. She was so fast. I didn't lose her until the highway. She chased me down the street!"

I could picture it all too clearly. I'd seen Mary move. She'd scuttled up those church steps far too fast. She'd kept time with me in the hall of the school without difficulty. The thought of her given free rein to run—an unstoppable force—made my muscles tense, my feet itch to escape. All I wanted was to flee forever.

Cody dabbed at Jess's wounds with surprising gentleness. Dell limped toward the phone on the wall. "Did you warn your parents, Jessica?"

Jess nodded, or tried to. It was more a head jerk. "Dad knows. He's taking Mom and Todd away. He told me to come here."

"Wait, what?" Jess had been adamant that none of us tell our parents, but hers had known all along? *How was that fair?* I scowled at her.

"My dad knows but not my mom," Jess explained between snivels. "She'd never understand."

"All Worths know their monster, Shauna. Including my nephew." Dell picked up the phone, her hands trembling around the receiver. Dell had lived with the threat of Bloody Mary all her life. What about this had her so worried?

"Wait," said Kitty. "If the glass is gone, how's Mary going to climb back in? Can't she go back through another mirror?"

Dell's fingers flew over the buttons on the phone. "I don't know. The only way to know for sure is to summon her."

"No." Kitty's answer was emphatic.

Dell's call had connected, and now I could see her pacing—or limping—back and forth, her hand waving excitedly as she spoke. Every few words her volume raised enough that I caught a snippet. I heard Elsa once, which piqued my interest, but Dell immediately grew quiet again, keeping the conversation private.

"If it's the only way to see if Mary's back in the mirror, we have to," Cody said. "We'll salt the hell out of it. We know what to do."

"No, no, and no!" Kitty stomped her foot so hard, the tchotchkes in the curio clattered and Horace sprinted for the steps and disappeared upstairs. "It's bad enough we have Mary's current victim here, but Jess is also a Worth girl. It's different this time. Mary's twice as obsessed. I signed up for putting her away, not for getting killed."

"You've been through enough, Kitty," Jess said softly. "The rest of you don't have to do it, either. This is pointless."

Jess believed her death was a foregone conclusion. I'd told myself I wouldn't care if Mary ate Jess alive, piece by piece, for what she'd done to Anna. The truth was more complicated. I wanted to fight for the friend I had for all those years. Not the person she turned out to be, but the person I thought I knew.

"Jess, come on. We'll find something," I said. "Your aunt is in the kitchen right now trying to figure it out. She knows a lot about Mary."

Jess's paper-thin smile was as convincing as my tone. "Sure. Thanks."

Finished with her call, Aunt Dell hobbled back to Jess's chair, shooing Cody away so she could inspect the injuries. Her finger wove into Jess's clumpy hair, parting it so she could look at the gash below. "It's not deep. No stitches. A compress and a bandage. Do you think you're well enough to summon Mary, Jessica?"

Jess shrugged. Dell grabbed her under the arm, hauling her to her feet. "We're not giving up. I called in a favor to Jonas Hawthorne about the Samburg girl. Something like this happened when Elsa was haunted. The girls ran from Mary when she pulled herself through the glass. They managed to get outside of the house. Mary chased them for a while. Obviously she went back in later, but I don't know the circumstances behind it. I'd like to ask Elsa directly if possible."

"Like, of the Hawthorne Hawthornes?" Cody asked. "Why would he know anything about Elsa Samburg?"

"There are a lot of Hawthornes in Solomon's Folly, Miss Jackson. Solomon dealt with the devil to ensure his family line would prosper. Jonas is the sheriff. His wife shares a room with Elsa Samburg in the assisted living facility. They're friends of a fashion. Maybe he can get us in. His blood owes mine, and I'm not afraid to remind him of that."

Dell guided Jess toward the bathroom, looping her arm around Jess's waist. I wasn't ready to follow them, not when they pushed open the door, not when Dell went to retrieve the summoning supplies. I didn't want to summon Mary any more than Kitty did.

"When you say he dealt with the devil, what do you mean?" Cody called out after Dell.

Dell emerged from the kitchen with a big box of salt clutched to her chest. She glanced from Cody to me and scowled. "Some things you're better off not knowing."

11

I couldn't bring myself to follow.

I stayed with Kitty in the living room, waiting for the others to finish the preparations. They'd done everything possible to ward the space: salted the mirror, taken down all the picture frames, and covered the chrome bath fixtures with masking tape.

It didn't feel adequate, but then, what would?

"Having Jess in front of the mirror should be enough," Kitty insisted from the couch. "It's bait. Why can't we try that?"

My eyes stayed pinned on the bathroom doorway. "I tried it weeks ago when Mom was there. Mary stayed away. It's not reliable. The summoning is."

It wasn't what Kitty wanted to hear. "Can they do it with three? Why does it have to be four?"

"Mary had four tormenters. I'm guessing it has to be four

to re-create what happened in the basement." I wanted to help the women in the other room, but I wouldn't risk another Mary tag. There was shame to the admission; if Cody could do it after seventeen years of haunting, I should have had the courage to follow in her footsteps.

But I didn't.

Mary's unleashed.

She was bad enough inside the glass. But free to wreak 150 years' worth of wrathful havoc? Catastrophe. We still didn't know what fueled her—blind rage at her unjust death or something else entirely. We didn't know how to stop her. All we had were puzzle pieces that barely fit together. A necklace buried in the church. A cast of villains so long dead, information about them was scarce. A family bloodline plagued by the ghost. The mystery of Hannah Worth's grave.

"She'll butcher people," I murmured. "Mary will pull them apart like Barbie dolls." She'd have a mountain of victims. A junkyard of patch parts. The old ghost would be a new ghost—a Frankenstein-esque abomination no one knew how to kill.

The bathroom door swung open. Out walked Cody, her frustration written on her face.

"Will one of you help with this? If not, we have to find someone."

I'd said I couldn't do it, but I have to. Kitty will. She'll go. No more Kitty on the chopping block. No more sacrificial friends.

"I'll go." I blurted it out before my wavering courage escaped me. I followed Cody into the bathroom, my legs feeling leaden.

Kitty called after me, but I ignored her and closed the door, blocking her from the imminent danger.

The click of the lock sent my heart racing. I braced myself against the side of the sink, my fear so potent my head spun.

Focus. You can do this. Breathe in. Breathe out.

The bathroom wasn't much to look at. Flat aqua paint above marbled white tiles. A linoleum floor lifting at the corners. Across from the door was a footed bathtub with no shower. The right wall had an alcove for towels and a hamper. Opposite that was a tiny hand mirror over the sink, disproportionate for the space but understandable if you lived with Mary. The toilet was tucked between the sink and bathtub. A pink pillar candle flickered beside the faucet, wax dripping down the sides to pool on the countertop.

Cody shoved me into the corner, between the wall and the end of the tub. She was to my left with the door at her back. Dell was to my right next to the toilet. Jess was front and center with the mirror. She looked exhausted. Dell had bandaged her head so it would stop bleeding, but the rest of her was as battered as before, her clothes torn almost beyond recognition.

Cody flicked off the light switch, plunging us into darkness.

The mirror an endless, black abyss. The glass thick but passable, allowing Mary to slip between worlds. My body hooked like a fish on a wire, Mary's claws spearing into me. Lungs tight and starved for air. Mouth opening and taking what should have been a last breath, only to swallow an ocean of cold, brackish water. Drowning. No sound. No light. Total nothingness.

"Stay with us, Shauna," Dell said. "You'll be all right."

She and Cody clutched my hands—I wasn't sure if that was because they wanted to keep me upright or keep me trapped. I knew there was no way I was leaving until the summoning was complete.

"Get it over with," Cody snapped. She sounded mad, but her hand fluttered against mine.

She's as scared as I am, I thought. Cody's fear helped me wrestle my own panic. *I'm okay. We're all okay. We know what we're doing.*

"Let's do this," I rasped. "Before I remember how dumb this is."

Jess's voice was tight. "Will she even come? I thought it had to be teenagers."

"Childless women," Dell said. "Age is unimportant."

The candlelight flickered over Jess's swollen face. She looked like an extra in a zombie film, the bruises going from red to purple at the middle.

"Bloody Mary. Bloody Mary. Bloody Mary." Her voice rang out like a bell.

My head whipped toward the mirror. A line of salt along the bottom frame. Crisscrossing tape across the middle, more salt ensuring Mary couldn't jam anything bigger than a finger or two through the glass. It was strange the way the tape fractured our shadowy reflections. Jess was an eye, a swollen lip, a chin. Cody was a tuft of hair and a nose.

Jess repeated the summons. "Bloody Mary. Bloody Mary. Bloody Mary."

The glass stayed firm and dark. No spectral fog. No condensation. No ambling figure moving our way from a swampy distance. It should have been a relief that we'd failed, but it was another reason for worry. Four women all tied to Bloody Mary, all bled by her, some of us feeding her our body parts, and she couldn't bother to come.

Why? Because she's no longer behind the glass to hear our call.

If we can't soften the glass to send her back, how do we get rid of her?

⤬

"It changes nothing," Kitty insisted as we walked back to the car. She had a scrap of paper in hand—directions for a rendezvous point outside of the Hockomock. Cody followed us, but Dell and Jess would meet us after Jess took a shower and changed. "Okay, wait. It might change one thing. Do we really have to go find Hannah? What are we even looking for again?"

"Hannah's important," Cody insisted. "Mary won't attack a girl in front of a mother. We have to assume that's because of Mary's feeling toward her own mother. I still won't rule out the possibility that Starkcrowe, or whoever, killed Hannah and Mary both. If that's the case, why wouldn't he put their bodies together? Especially if Hannah's so out of the way. Mary wasn't in the church. She has to be somewhere. It's worth the look."

"I hate everything about this," Kitty said. "I don't want to dig for any more bodies. I don't want to work with Jess."

Cody grumbled and swatted at herself, striking the side of

her neck. She kept slapping at the spot until her peach skin turned red. More imaginary bugs. "None of us do, but we suck it up. Her aunt's the best line on information we have, and if Mary really isn't in the glass anymore, Jess poses no threat. She's on our side."

Kitty got into the car, slammed the door, and tossed the directions my way. "Jess is on no one's side but her own. We can't trust her."

I reached out to squeeze her arm. She offered me a wan smile that didn't reach her eyes. "I know how you feel, but Cody's right. We need Aunt Dell. We have to tolerate Jess if we want to pursue Mary," I said.

Kitty bit her tongue and started driving. I pulled out the Mary notebook, writing about the necklace, the Worth girl history, and what Mary did to those she'd taken. I felt like everything I needed to know to stop Mary was right there in front of me, but I was missing the thread that tied it all together.

"I'd really like to find out why the pastor married Elizabeth Hawthorne," I said. "That has to be significant. None of Mary's letters suggested they were involved, and Joseph's letter made it sound like Elizabeth didn't go into the marriage willingly. Maybe Dell can ask the sheriff for some of their family stuff."

Cody grunted. "I'd like to look at the rest of Dell's collection. We barely saw anything. My cousin's missing person's report was in there. Was she keeping track of Mary's victims? I'll be curious to hear what Elsa Samburg has to say about everything, too, though I've heard she's crazier than a bucket of drunk monkeys."

The roads worsened the farther along we went, going from paved to dirt, from straight to twisty. At first there were houses and stores around us, then only houses. Eventually, trees, shrubs, and thick undergrowth were our only companions. Kitty drove until there was no road left to drive. The way was barred by two rusted-out chains stretched between a pair of oak trees. The NO TRESPASSING sign was vandalized with so much red spray paint, it was hard to see the warning underneath.

"Charming." I climbed from the car. A mosquito buzzed at my ear. I smacked it away as Cody pulled out insect repellant. She sprayed herself and handed me the bottle. I turned to offer it to Kitty, but she was still in the car, slouched against her seat with her eyes closed.

Kitty cracked open the door as I approached.

"Do you need to go home?" I asked. "It's okay."

"I'm not going anywhere." She wouldn't look at me, instead concentrating on the felt roof of the SUV. "I know I have to deal with Jess. I don't like it. It scares me. It's like walking around with a grenade in my pocket. Cody said she isn't a threat, but why would Mary stop following Jess just because she's out of the mirror?"

Cody sensed we needed a moment alone. She wandered down the dirt road, pausing every few feet to pick up rocks and chuck them into the swamp. "Mary hunts through the mirror,"

I said. "She smells us through the glass. It's a conduit. How's she going to find us without it?"

Kitty rolled her eyes. "If Mary's going to come anywhere, where do you think it will be? Solomon's Folly is her hometown. Don't tell me we're in less danger. *We're in more.*"

12

Dell showed up with a compass, a map, a fanny pack, and a pair of yellow duck boots that looked hideous with her velour track-suit. She exited Jess's car with purpose, sweeping the sides of the narrow road. Every few feet, she reached into the brush to pull out a stick. She'd check the length against her cane before either adding it to her growing collection or tossing it away.

Jess followed behind her in clothes too big for her frame. The blood was washed away, the worst of the cuts bandaged, but her face looked pulpy, as if she'd been boxing. Her sidelong glances suggested she had things to say to me, but Kitty's words had their hooks in me.

Don't tell me we're in less danger. We're in more.

Jess was a walking, talking target.

"How are you feeling?" I asked her. Kitty cast me a sideward glance that I pretended I didn't see.

"I hurt, but it's tolerable." She tried to smile at me but ended up cringing.

Her swollen lip. It hurts.

"Take it easy out there, then."

She nodded.

"What's with the sticks?" Cody called to Dell. "Are we building a fire?"

"No. Black Betty. Quicksand. Before you step anywhere, poke the ground to see if it's soft. We should watch for traps, too. People hunt here. The last thing any of us need is a foothold trap going off."

"Foothold traps. Like bear traps? You're serious?" Kitty's face screwed up in horror, but Dell was too busy gathering to notice.

"Oh, yes. This is a hunters' road. Jessica's father used to trap muskrats here as a teenager. Watch your footing and stay together and we'll be fine. But we'll want to get out before dark. Too many unsavory things come out at night." Dell handed us our sticks as if she was distributing Halloween candy, tucking one into each of our fists with a smile.

"If Hannah was buried near the church, why did we have to get on the highway?" I asked, following Dell past the rusty chains and toward a thicket of trees and waist-tall grass. She pulled out her compass, oriented herself, and forged ahead. She didn't move fast, but nobody would in a place like this. The ferns were up to my knees. Moss covered the tree trunks around me, and four steps in, I had thorns tugging at my pant leg.

Dell snapped off a branch that barred our way. Her walking

stick poked out, nudging at the ground before she pressed deeper into the swamp. "We're coming at it from the other side of the river. Hannah wasn't allowed near the church. Suicides were considered unworthy of holy ground. Women who died in childbirth, too—they were unclean."

At first, the path wasn't clear, but the farther we explored, the more obvious it became. Our sliver of dirt had less over-growth than our surroundings. Dell was our fearless leader, followed by me, Kitty, Cody, and finally Jess. I prodded with my stick, pausing every time the earth squished. I thought quick-sand was an exotic, tropical problem—not something you'd find in New England.

The canopy above was so thick the sunlight barely pierced through. It cast everything in a dank pallor, thickening the shadows and hiding the very swamp floor we needed to fear. The air smelled like fresh-turned dirt and water, the moisture mak-ing my clothes stick to my body. Every few minutes a bullfrog croaked or birds cawed in the trees, but otherwise it was quiet.

Except for the clanging.

Clunk. Clunk. Clunk.

Whatever was inside Jess's backpack dinged with each step. Or maybe it was the shovel on her shoulder striking the side of the backpack.

"What's the shovel for?" I asked.

"Hannah," she said. "Dell told me to bring it."

Kitty groaned. "We're not digging her up. I said no grave robbing, and I meant it."

"It's not grave robbing if we take nothing. It's unearthing

the truth," Dell said. "You don't have to participate, Kitty. You can go back to the ca—"

"Don't say that!" Kitty stopped so abruptly, Cody walked into her. Jess had to take a step back so she didn't accidentally impale anyone with the shovel. I reached for Dell's sleeve, tugging it so she'd pause.

Kitty addressed all of us. "Just because I bring up a concern doesn't mean I want to go home. I'm afraid, but I'm staying. I don't want to see any more dead people, but I'll go with you because I want Mary gone. I'd really appreciate someone explaining why we're about to dig up Mary Worth's dead mother, though, because, like, this is messed up. Totally messed up."

Dell didn't answer with words, just a gesture. She unzipped the fanny pack, ignoring the cell phone, house keys, and pill bottle to produce a folded piece of paper. It was another photocopied letter, but it was incomplete, the top portion indiscernible thanks to water stains and ink blobs. I'd seen the writing on the lower half before, though—Joseph Simpson. I took it from her, skimming past the smudges to the first complete line.

—he recalls little about the location beyond the cave. His instructions were to bury her somewhere the animals wouldn't disturb the remains. We know he set out from the church and went across the river into the swamp. That took him southwest.

I've asked Mister Winters to accompany me. He makes his livelihood hunting in the swamp. He thinks the cave is near Samoset's Perch. I have no idea what that means, but I follow in hopes of finding your sister. If Mrs. Carroll's account is true, the figure she saw may have been Mary looking for your mother.

"Do you know who Mrs. Carroll is? Or where Samoset's Perch is?" I handed the letter to Cody, who read it and handed it to Kitty. Jess declined, maintaining her silence at the back of the pack. The letter passed up the line and back to Dell.

She tucked it into her fanny pack. "There's no other mention of a Mrs. Carroll in any other letters I've read. I'm assuming she's a townswoman. I mentioned before we came here when Elsa had the ghost. We had to leave early because of swamp gas, but I saw the cave entrance as we ran out. I haven't had a good enough reason to come back until now." Dell barged through a pair of overgrown shrubs, surprisingly spry considering her years and the impediment. I could picture her in a safari hat slashing at the flora with a machete.

"Swamp gas?" Kitty repeated, still incredulous. "That's a thing? I mean, I believe you, but it's so messed up."

"Phantom fog," Cody said. "It's greenish. If you see it, you run or it sweeps you away and we'll be reading your obituary in a week."

Kitty's moan sounded as if she'd stepped in one of the traps Dell had warned us about. "You want me to believe in killer fog."

Cody snorted. "No, I want you and Shauna to get your heads on straight. Mary's not the end of the weird shit around here. She's the beginning. And if we say run, you'd better run."

Dell paused to check the compass, her hand batting at a cloud of flies hovering near her face. "We go east from here. If you see a stream, let me know. Samoset's Perch will be nearby. It's tallish and hard to miss." She bullied her way through another patch of tall grass, using her walking cane to pry a thick log from our path.

"What's the significance of Samoset's Perch?" I asked, crouching to help her. The log was wet and covered in green algae and moss, with feathery layers of mushrooms along the top. The moment I touched it, ants exploded from the ends to swarm over my hands. I chucked it and slapped the insects away.

Mary's beetles on your skin. Scurry, scurry under your clothes and into your hair. All over with their threadlike legs and gnashy pinchers.

"Nasty."

Dell cast me a sympathetic look before pressing on. "Samoset's Perch is a rise in the swamp named after the Wampanoag who met the English settlers when they arrived in Plymouth. Some say it's where Solomon first declared the land his, but I'm not sure I believe that. It'd be settled otherwise. There'd be more construction."

"There's some," Cody said. "You'll find gutted houses in places. Nothing intact enough to let people live there, but the building foundations are around. We used to play in them as kids."

Dell grunted but said nothing.

A glance at my phone told me forty minutes had passed since we'd left the car. The path was barely recognizable anymore, and the swamp grew less inviting with the addition of a new, invasive plant. It covered everything—the ground, the bottoms of the trees, and the darkest, shadowy bits under the rocks.

I pointed at it. "This isn't poison oak, right?"

"Peat moss," Cody said. "We're in bog land. Your cranberries come from somewhere."

"Oh." I felt dumb, but at least I wouldn't have to stress about getting a rash all over my legs.

A few minutes later, Dell gestured to our right. The stream. It wound around a cluster of saplings before veering off. It wasn't particularly big, maybe five feet across, the water no more than two feet at its deepest point. There was a separation at the middle, a lichen-covered rock forcing a fork, where a turtle with a shell as big around as a bicycle tire sunned itself.

Dell angled toward the stream, her stick still poking at the ground to see if it would give. "Snapper. Avoid her. Those jaws can and will sever fingers."

"This place keeps getting better and better," Kitty grumbled.

We followed Dell past the hissing turtle and along the stream bank, taking side paths to avoid the nastier terrain. At one point, Dell jabbed the earth and found it squishy-soft, like gritty pudding. She threw out her arm to stop us from walking past her, carefully maneuvering us to solid ground, between the dead leaves, the moss, and the network of vines stretching between the trees.

The stream led us farther into the swamp. Not too much later, I could make out a jutting rock formation on the horizon. It wasn't as big as I expected, its peak not quite meeting the treetops.

Dell whooped.

"Jessica, up here with me. We want the flashlights."

Jess shuffled past us to join her aunt. The two of them eased their way down a steep slope and toward the perch. The cave wasn't hard to find. A pair of boulders bordered a recess in the earth, the back wall formed by Samoset's Perch itself. The entrance was round and wide, the stalactites along the top looking like fangs inside a gaping maw. Such an evil place could snap shut and swallow us down forever.

"She could be out here?" I offered weakly.

Eight eyes turned to me.

If she's anywhere she's inside, and we all know it.

13

Crossing from the outside world into the cave depths was like opening the house door after a snowstorm: warm on one side, biting on the other. Kitty huddled into my side, the two of us following Dell and Jess's lantern with chattering teeth. Our one victory was that nothing flew at our heads.

"How far down are we going?" Cody asked from behind me. When I turned to look at her, she was a silhouette in the dark, the light occasionally flashing over the whites of her eyes. It made me think of Peter Pan's shadow claiming children for Neverland.

"I don't know. I won't go too much deeper, though. It narrows ahead." I couldn't see Dell, but I trusted her because I had to. Without her, I was lost in the middle of a killer swamp.

"Look over there," Jess said, her voice raspy. Almost like Cody's. Dell swung us to the right, taking the light with her. My hand latched onto the back of her jacket. Jess stepped aside to let the rest of us see the alcove. The ceiling was about five feet high. Moss blanketed the ground and walls, long-stemmed tufts of it growing from the cracks in the stone. Across the middle of the floor stretched a flat column of small, stacked rocks. At the head of the pile was a larger rock that could have easily been a makeshift headstone.

"Do you think—"

"Yes," Dell said, cutting off Cody. "Jessica, shovel."

Jess offered it to her aunt, accepting Dell's cane in response. Dell limped over to the pile, using the pointed side of the shovel to unearth the rocks. She had to break through a crust of the moss to get to them, but soon they rolled away, exposing more rocks underneath. And more rocks under that. I didn't expect the elder among us to be the one to take on the physical labor, but something spurred her.

Kitty couldn't watch. She turned away to study the rest of the cave, not that she could see anything with the flashlights pointed in the opposite direction. She jogged in place to keep her temperature up, the legs of her jeans swishing.

My attention fixed on Dell. The uppermost rocks were easy to dislodge, but it got harder once she started going into the ground itself. She'd spear the shovel in and then have to take a breath before hoisting the dirt away.

"Can I help?" I offered.

Dell motioned me near. "There's water down there. It's making mud, and mud is heavy. I doubt there will be much left, but maybe we can find a clue or two, like the necklace. I know it's a long shot, but we came all the way here and I doubt they dug too deep. Not for a woman the pastor deemed worthless."

I dug. Moving the sodden earth strained my back, but I kept at it, grunting each time I heaved a shovel full of dirt and rocks aside. The water came faster, filling the recess as I cleared mud out. I worked from the bottom part of the rock pile up, keeping everything level. There was an odor on the air that hadn't been there before we opened up the ground. It wasn't rot like Mary, but something sour and salty. Like low tide on the ocean.

"I can't believe we're doing this," Kitty murmured. "It's sick."

"You're not doing anything. Just standing there." Cody sounded annoyed.

"Leave her alone." I turned back to the task at hand. "She's right to think this is disgusting. Because it is."

"It's necessary." Cody approached the hole, crouching to peer into the large rectangle. Her hand swiped through the water. Her head tilted. "There's something under here. Something not dirt."

I tapped her sneaker with the edge of the shovel. "Disgusting and necessary aren't mutually exclusive. Move. You're in my light."

Cody smacked the shovel away. "Did someone bring a bucket? Something we can use to get the water out."

Jess dug through the backpack. She produced a stack of plastic cups, the red kind people used for soda at parties. "We brought them for drinking water, but here." Cody snatched them from her, going back at the hole to remove two cups of muddy water at a time. Dell edged nearer with her flashlight; Jess, too. Only Kitty stood off to the side, still refusing to watch.

She was the only one who didn't see the face in the water.

Hannah Worth was supposed to be dust and bones at 150 years dead. But what we unearthed were not dry, skeletal remains. The body was wet. Flesh plumped the cheeks, a discernable curvature to the lips. Her features were as plain as they were in the photographs I'd seen just hours ago.

Hannah Worth was *juicy* inside of her watery grave.

In life, Hannah was a beautiful woman with ivory skin and golden hair. The peaty bog had left her the color of soot, but there was no denying her identity. Her eyes were closed, the corners crinkled like she'd squeezed them shut. A delicately arched nose, high cheekbones. Some kind of wrap covered her hair, made of leather or soft cloth. It fastened underneath her chin in a bow. It, too, had not gone to rot.

I stumbled away from the body, my hand held up as if I was afraid she'd rise from the dead and strike me. How was it possible? I could have understood if we'd found nothing, but to discover something so disturbingly untouched after all that time—I couldn't process it.

I stifled a shriek into the back of my arm, staring at Dell and waiting for answers, but she had none. Her fingers were pressed to her mouth, her eyes wide. Jess leaned into her aunt's side, the lift of her brows telling me she was as freaked-out as the rest of us.

Cody shook her head, still crouched next to the hole, her mouth opening and closing in astonished disbelief.

"What's going on over there?" Kitty demanded. "What's wrong?"

"She barely looks dead," I managed despite my shock.

Kitty still danced to keep warm, but that made her go stock-still. "What?"

"No other way to explain it. She looks like she just died. She's discolored—blackened, like leather—but I can see a mole on her temple. She has a mole." Cody pointed at a small growth beneath her hairline. Time had robbed her of few of the finer details.

Jess eased out from behind Dell, moving to my side in the dark. Her fingers brushed my wrist, but I was too stunned to pull away. "How? Is she a vampire or something?"

Dell let out a long breath, like she hadn't exhaled in days. "N-no. I've read of things like this. Bog men. Bog corpses. If you're buried in salt water, or near salt water, and there's peat . . . Jesus Christ. Pardon me. It's shock. Right. At least we know she's buried alone. Mary would have been on top of her if they were in a double grave. She died second."

"She didn't drown," Cody said. "There's no way she drowned. He did it—Starkcrowe—or if he didn't, someone else did."

"How do you know that?" I looked from Cody to the corpse, the water covering only half of Hannah's ears, her face pointed at the cave ceiling. "How can you tell?"

"Her eyes are closed, like she knew it was coming. Also, if she'd been in the river, her features wouldn't be so perfect. Rivers have tides. Tides lash at the face. Water corpses also bloat. Look at her."

"How do you know all this stuff?" I asked, incredulous. Cody looked embarrassed for a moment, but she shrugged her shoulders like she could slough it off. She then proceeded to smack at her neck, at bugs she felt but no one could see.

"There wasn't much I could do when I was in the house alone. The social worker brought me library books."

I slid down the cave wall to sit on my butt, my feet stopping short of the grave. "If what Cody's saying is true, there's no evidence of drowning in the river. The account of Hannah's death was totally made up. That's another reason Mary has to be so mean."

Dell moved away from the body, pausing by Jess and holding out her hand for her walking stick, tears running down her cheeks. "I'm going to call Jonas and see what he suggests. I dislike disturbing the dead any more than we already have, but she deserves a real burial. Mary would have thought so, I think. Cover her as gently as possible, please. Dirt only, no rocks."

Looking at Hannah, I could see the sordid beginning of Mary's hate spiral.

Kitty went with Dell outside, leaving me, Cody, and Jess to rebury Hannah. I almost asked if we should take a picture for research purposes, but that felt more irreverent than unearthing her in the first place. Covering her was far quicker than digging for her. We used our hands to push the dirt back into the hole, careful to abide by Dell's wishes. Outside, Dell and Kitty stood elbow to elbow, both peering up at Samoset's Perch.

"Jonas is sending the deputy for Hannah. They'll call the coroner to be sure she's taken care of. I have room in the family plot for her. Maybe a proper blessing will put Mary at peace." Dell looked down from the rocks to force a smile, motioning back at the stream with her cane. "He can get you girls in to see Elsa in the morning, but he'd like to meet with you tonight, at the farmhouse. I'll give you directions after dinner."

"You're not going?" Jess asked.

"No, and neither are you. The last time I saw Elsa, she had a reaction. She has a talent that I . . . It's like she senses Mary's taint, and Worth women are tainted. You're staying with me. The other three have a much better chance at communicating without you there."

Jess didn't look pleased, but she didn't argue.

We fell into line to make our way back to the car. It was quiet except for the rustling of leaves and the furious hum of mosquitoes. I didn't realize how tired I was until we had to scale the slope instead of slide down it. Kitty went up first and offered me a hand. With her help, I forced my way to the top, my thighs and back aching with every step. When I pulled away from her, dirt smeared her palm. I was slathered in mud from fingertips to elbow, the guck stiffening my jeans and browning my sneakers.

Cody and Jess had just pulled Dell up with the rest of us

when a scream blasted through the trees. It was loud and high-pitched, more a shriek than a wail. The birds exploded from their nests in fear and agitation. A flock swooped down at us, so low I could feel the air pressure of their wing beats.

"What the hell was that?" Kitty demanded.

Cody grabbed her by the elbow only to take off at a dead run. "Mary!"

14

She's coming.

Get away. Get as far away as you can.

The trees shivered, the leaves whispering with the breeze. A snap in the brush sent me scurrying ahead, but I didn't run off, not with Dell struggling to keep pace behind me. It would have been easy to abandon her and Jess, but getting lost in a place with phantoms, quicksand, and wild dogs sounded almost as bad as facing Mary.

I looked ahead, at Kitty's disappearing pastel-colored dot.

Kitty! Wait for me, please! Don't leave me behind.

She kept running.

It was strange to be in such an open area and to feel so trapped. The shrubs, saplings, and vines closed in. I couldn't step too far to the left for fear of traps. Too far to the right, Black Betty. Another ghostly cry blasted through the swamp. I ran to the stream, my heart pounding like a timpani drum.

I spotted Cody's slate-blue sweatshirt and Kitty's pink tee at the fork. Kitty stumbled back, her stick beating the ground in front of her.

"Jump over it," Cody snapped. Except Cody didn't move ahead either, eyeing the turtle that had relocated from her rock perch to the path. The turtle's head extended from her shell, beaked mouth agape and hissing. Black mud blanketed her except for her eyes, which shone like polished beads in her leathery skin.

"This is stupid." Cody sidestepped the turtle, only to have the ground gulp down her foot as soon as she put her weight on it. Sand clutched her sneaker, slurping on the dingy white leather. Kitty's last-second grab stopped Cody from falling face-first into the hidden pit.

"Holy shit!" Cody scampered back as the turtle lunged, another sibilant hiss warning us away from the territory she'd claimed. Kitty jabbed at her with her thick stick, but the turtle's jaws clamped on the end and snapped it off.

"South!" Dell called from some yards back. "Follow the stream."

"We can't. Turtle and quicksand." Cody retreated, her stick searching the ground for patches of hungry earth but finding none.

"Then it's detour time." Dell turned and led us deeper into the Hockomock, away from the straight trajectory and into a tangle of leaves, vines, ferns, and bushes. We struggled with every step through the dense undergrowth. Kitty kept stepping on the heels of my shoes, but it wasn't her fault. There was simply no place else for her to go.

We kept going until we hit a thick wall of shrubs. A steep drop-off to the right and a patch of soggy earth to the left. It was through the shrubs or turn back. Dell shoved at the branches with her cane, but she didn't make much headway. I stepped in to take her place, using my body as a battering ram. I pierced the first layer of shrubs and pressed into the second.

"Come with me, or they'll close," I said. Kitty followed, then Cody, Jess, and Dell. Sandwiched as I was, I couldn't see the ground, but if the shrubs weren't sinking, neither were we. I pressed forward, emerging into a glen with an arranged ring of rocks at the center. The remains of a long-abandoned fire were scattered across the dirt. Rusty cages formed a lopsided pyramid off to the right, a mildewed wooden rack half-collapsed from years of disuse behind them.

Samoset's Perch, the stream, the path—everything familiar was hidden by a sentry line of oak trees tall enough to touch the sky. Their roots rose up from the ground like a nest of roiling tentacles, their trunks so thick around, they were four people wide.

"A hunter's camp?" Kitty asked.

"Looks like it," I said.

Jess helped pull Dell from the shrubs' clutching branches. A fresh cut bled along Dell's jaw, but she paid it no mind. She was too intent on pulling her compass from her fanny pack and orienting herself.

"Southeast, if any of you have compasses." I didn't, but I did have a phone. As Dell retook the lead, I checked my cell, surprised to discover four-bar reception in the middle of a swamp. Kitty guided me along at a stumble while I opened the app on my phone.

I'd pulled up the compass dial on my screen when I heard a snap followed by a howl. Kitty stopped dead. I slammed into her back, my free hand bracing against her shoulder. Three feet in front of us, Cody bent over at the waist, her arms wrapped around her middle. The color had drained from her face; her single eye drizzled tears. She teetered back and forth, rocking on her heels. I didn't understand why until I looked down.

White sneaker gone red.

Oh, no. Oh, God, no.

The trap clamped on the end of her sneaker, the metal teeth buried deep into the soft leather.

"Get it off of me," Cody rasped.

We were statues in a gallery, poised but unmoving. Cody's whistling squeal, reminding me of a kettle left to boil, ripped Dell from her stupor. She offered Cody the cane, but not before Cody collapsed to the ground, forcing the trap to tilt back with her. I saw jaws and a metal chain spiked into the ground. Unlike the rusty cages, it gleamed silver.

Dell crouched to sling an arm around Cody's shoulders. Jess knelt on the other side, reaching for the trap. She paused when Cody cried into a wad of her sweatshirt. The muffled sobs broke my heart; Cody was the strong, salty one. She was the warrior. Her tears were a foreboding omen.

So was the shrill cry of a furious Mary. Another blast of birds careened past us, their survival instincts telling them to flee, flee, flee! Every part of me wanted to run with them, but I couldn't abandon Cody.

"Sorry," Jess mumbled, grabbing the trap and prying it open, her arms quivering with the strain. The jaws parted an inch, but then Jess's fingers slid through the blood slicking the stainless steel. It slipped from her grasp. *SNAP!* A second bite into Cody's foot. Cody screamed, her temples covered in sweat, the pool of blood spreading. It stained her jeans, climbing from frayed hem to ankle and rising to her calf.

Jess set her jaw, her eyes rimmed red. She tried again. Her fingers shook as she forced open the sides, her thumb and forefinger hooked in such a way that if Cody got bit, Jess's fingers were fodder, too. She shuddered, all her strength concentrated on freeing Cody. She peeled the mouth open another inch, far enough that Cody's foot could slip out if it wasn't impaled. I dashed in to help, lifting Cody's sneaker from the bottom teeth before maneuvering her foot down and away from the top ones. She came free with another chorus of whimpers.

Kitty figured out how the trap worked. She waited for me to move Cody aside before stepping on the springs on either side of the jaws, forcing the mechanisms to click into place. The mouth of the trap stopped biting, and Jess jerked her hands away, her arms slick with Cody's blood.

"Go," Cody growled, huddled against Dell's chest. "I'll slow you down." Blood bubbled up through the gouges in her sneaker like a crimson geyser.

"No," Dell said, speaking for all of us. "If anyone will peel off, it will be me and Jessica. I'm old and slow. Jessica is marked. You have a fair shot of getting out of here."

My eyes searched the trees. I kept expecting to see Mary's haggard, gray face peering out at us, but nothing.

Yet.

"We need to move," Jess said, wiping her bloody hands on her jeans. "It's not safe here."

"She's right. Get her up." Dell took a deep breath and pried off Cody's sneaker. Cody kept flinching, so Dell looped an arm around her lower leg to hold her still. I wanted to shout at Dell to go faster, *didn't she know what was coming for us*, but it was delicate work. Cody keened as the sneaker pulled away, her sock so saturated with blood it was black. Perspiration dripped from her temples while dark sweat rings formed under her arms.

Dell wobbled on her haunches, her hand clamping on my knee to stop herself from falling.

"How is your leg?" I asked.

"It hurts, but it's manageable. I'm lucky it hasn't given out." Dell stripped down to an old tank top, using her track jacket to fashion a tourniquet. The sleeves tied above Cody's ankle, the rest swaddling the injured foot. As soon as Dell pushed away, Kitty hooked an arm around Cody's waist, bracing to take her weight.

I took Cody's other side, squatting to help her up. Cody wasn't big, but Kitty and I strained to get her off the ground. She held her foot up as we trudged along, Dell leading the pack. We moved southeast, scaling hills that looked gentle but proved challenging with Cody's additional weight. Dell paused before we dipped into a valley between two taller inclines, the furrow in the ground watery and bristled with ferns. She tilted her head back to look at the canopy. Her eyes closed and she sucked in a breath.

"It's quiet," she said.

No wind. No frogs or crickets or birds. It was perfectly still in a place that had no business being still.

"She's here," Jess said. "Mary's here."

15

Mary blended into the trees. A decrepit dead girl ought to call more attention to herself, but the shadows were thick and the dirt smearing her clothes acted as camouflage. My manifested nightmare, five yards away. Staring. Waiting.

Her skull was more pronounced than I remembered. A pointed head covered by bulging black veins, the gray skin so thin along her cheekbones I caught glimpses of skull. A noseless void at the center of her face, receding lips exposing moldy gums and broken yellow teeth that looked as if they'd been filed to points. Her hair had fallen out except for a few dark strands above her temples.

And her eyes...

Her *eye.*

The left one was as black and as recessed as our last encounter. But the right was different. Film covered the pupil, milky tendrils threading out toward the whites, but I could see the iris underneath. Honey golden brown with dark rings around the edges. I knew that eye. I'd seen it every day for three years *in someone else's head.*

Anna's eye.

I took a step back, but I was stuck, sagging beneath Cody's weight, far too close to Mary. "We should go," I whispered. "Now."

Mary stepped toward us. Her foot sloshed as it struck the ground, the flesh full like a balloon and bulbous at the ankle. It was engorged to the knee, where it appeared to taper, her dress hiding her thigh. Beetles darted in and out of the gashes covering her body. Lumplike shapes pressed on her skin from the inside as they wriggled to and fro.

Dell held her cane aloft like a sword. "Mary, we're here to help you. We found your moth—" Mary lunged for her, arms lashing out, fingers curled over as if she wanted to peel Dell's face from her skull. Her digits were spindly and bluish, but there were two that looked fresh—the ring finger beside the pinky was pink and plump, seamlessly blending into the rest of her parts. There'd been only one yesterday.

Dell whipped the cane around, bashing Mary upside the head. The ghost screeched, bumbling back and hissing like the turtle. "Run! Go south!" Dell shouted, whipping the cane around a second time, clobbering Mary in the knee. Mary growled, but she didn't fall, instead advancing on Dell with wet gurgles.

Kitty took off running, pulling me and Cody with her. We moved fast, but not fast enough with Cody dangling between us. Cody knew it, too.

"Leave me," Cody snarled, "I'm slowing you down."

Terror choked any reply I wanted to make.

GET OUT, GET OUT, GET OUT!

We ran blind, hoping with every step to avoid traps and quicksand. I held my phone with my free hand, the compass guiding us in the direction of the car. Behind us, Jess screamed. I whimpered, scared for her and Dell. Scared for me and Kitty and Cody, too. The fear was all-encompassing—it was the only thing that mattered anymore.

Kitty headed right to avoid passing through bramble bushes with thorns the size of my thumb. Around a pine tree, a boulder, and down a slope, toward a straightaway with knee-high plants and patchy grass. Her breath came in short pants, her face so sweaty that her hair stuck to her forehead and neck.

"I need a second," Kitty wheezed. "Asthma." We didn't have a second, but she couldn't breathe. We paused at the edge of the clearing, Cody clinging harder to me so Kitty could use her inhaler.

"This is stupid," Cody murmured. "You should leave me." Her head lolled forward as if the weight was too much for her neck to support, but then she jerked it back up again, refusing to stay down. I glanced at her wrapped foot. Cody wasn't just bleeding. She was bleeding *to death*.

Kitty crammed the inhaler into her pocket and readjusted Cody's weight across her shoulders. I readied for another sprint, but when I stepped forward, my foot wouldn't lift. I tried the other one. It was too heavy, as if drowned in cement. Black Betty. But it wasn't like Cody's earlier sinking—it was slower. More insidious.

Kitty squirmed on Cody's other side, thrashing as if she were on fire.

"Don't. You'll sink faster. Stay calm," Cody said, her voice so quiet I had to crane my neck to hear her.

I shoved the phone into my jeans pocket and went perfectly still, the sand up to my ankle. "Get Cody on the slope. We're not so far in we can't pull each other out."

Kitty bit her bottom lip, tears swelling in her eyes as we readjusted our grip on the slack woman between us. With a soft, quick countdown, we tossed Cody to safety. We tried to be gentle, but Cody hit the bank with a thud, cussing a blue streak when her foot struck the ground.

"Sorry!" Kitty reached out to grip my arm, like clinging to me would somehow stop her from being swallowed.

Cody rolled onto her hip. Pale and covered in sweat, she looked precariously close to shock. She reached out her hand for me. "It's not too deep. Grab on."

My grip locked on her forearm near her elbow, hers did the same. With Cody as an anchor, I pulled one foot from the grasping muck. There was a rude squelch as I came free. I extended my leg to the slope, and Cody heaved as best she could. I launched forward, landing on solid ground beside her.

I scrambled to my knees and offered my hands to Kitty. She leaned forward, going through the same process to free herself. On our feet, we flanked Cody's sides, lifting her from the ground with twin grunts. Cody whimpered as we moved her, her hold around our necks weaker than before.

We approached the bank, determined to scale it. Up one

step, up two. It wasn't an easy climb, but if we were slow and careful, we could get purchase to push onward. We were nearly to the top when I looked over the crest of the hillside and saw Mary sprinting our way, fresh blood splotching her dress across the bodice. She moved too fast, in a blur.

"Whose blood is that?" Kitty asked, rearing back and nearly toppling the three of us. I overcompensated by leaning forward, toward Mary despite every instinct.

"Kitty, *stop*. We'll end up in the quicksand again."

"She's coming," she warbled. "We have to run."

"Yes, but not that way. Up and around." We struggled up the incline despite the futility of the situation; we couldn't outrun Mary. We'd stabbed her and beaten her and inflicted all sorts of hurt on her, but she resurrected each time. In the past, salt sent Mary retreating into mirrors, but what mirrors did we have in a swamp?

I won't stand here and die. I won't hand over my friends.

Cody refused to be a hindrance.

As soon as we were on level ground, she fought us. I'd thought her strength diminished after the trap, but her fury was such that I had to let her go or get punched in the face. Kitty had a similar problem; Cody elbowed her in the gut over and over until she released her. As soon as she was free, she shoved my shoulders so hard, I stumbled back and into Kitty.

"Run," she growled. She reached into her jeans pocket and pulled out Mary's necklace, cramming it into my fist and curling my fingers over it. "There's a key under the mat behind the back door of my house. What's mine is yours. Finish it."

"Cody, what are you doi—"

"Run!" She screamed it in my face, spittle striking my cheeks as she pushed me a second time. I didn't argue as Kitty grabbed my hand and wrenched me back. The necklace dangled from my fingers.

"We're not leaving her," I insisted. "No!"

"We have to, Shauna!"

Cody whirled to meet Mary head-on, her weight balanced on her good foot. She lifted her chin and tore off the black patch, exposing the sewn-shut socket where her eye used to be. A mass of pink-and-white scar tissue covered her from brow to the side of her nose. She was as pale as paper and drenched with sweat. Her body trembled.

She'd never looked fiercer.

"I'M WAITING, MARY!"

Mary barreled our way, a shot fired from a gun. Kitty tried to steer me away, her fingers pinching my bicep, but my feet remained planted. *Cody*, I thought. *We have to help Cody.*

"Go," Cody implored. "I'm screwed anyway. Please." It was the *please* that did me in. I didn't want to abandon her, but we needed to persevere so Mary wouldn't haunt again. If Cody had to die to make it happen, that was her decision. I hated it, but it made sense. Cody made sense. Mary was too close for any other plan.

Twenty yards between us and Mary. Fifteen yards. Ten. I bumbled back, Kitty's grip tightening on my arm. Mary shrieked with fury before veering to the left—toward me and Kitty instead of Cody. *Two for the price of one*, I realized, delirious with terror. A bubble of crazed laughter threatened to burst from my mouth. Cody remained unfazed. She crouched low, her hand swiping out to close around a fist-sized rock.

"BLOODY MARY, BLOODY MARY, BLOODY MARY!" she mocked, her voice as strong as I'd ever heard it.

The ghoul's trajectory immediately changed, the taunt too personal to overlook. She launched herself at Cody, pouncing like a wolf on its prey. Her hands struck Cody's shoulders, her weight knocked Cody back. I screamed as they rolled down the hill, wrestling like cats the entire way. Mary thrashed and punished with those razor-tipped fingers. Cody returned the violence with the rock in her fist, hitting Mary on the back of the head over and over again. They rolled back and forth; sometimes Mary was on top. Sometimes Cody.

Screams, snarls, and sobs. The last were mine.

"Let's go," Kitty pleaded. "She's doing this for us."

Still I didn't move. Not until I saw the ground opening up, the sand rising. I understood then what Cody intended—to pull Mary under the quicksand. For a heartbeat, she looked up at the slope, her face covered with fresh cuts and blood. Somehow, despite the ghoul beneath her snarling, she found a smile for me. A big toothy one that stretched across the lower half of her face.

It was enough. I took Kitty's hand and we ran.

16

We kept going until our legs hurt and then until they didn't hurt.

Cody is dead. She saved us.

Kitty never let me go, her fingers laced with mine. I'd pocketed the necklace so I wouldn't lose it, retrieving my cell phone in its place. "Southeast" was the only direction we had to go on. We'd been cautious getting to Hannah, but the retreat was chaos with Mary in the swamp. Even if Cody dragged her down into the sand, who was to say she'd stay there? Who was to say Mary didn't finish Cody and crawl out before she drowned?

We smashed our way through another thicket and toward a flat glen peppered with spicebushes and low-growing bittersweet. I let go of Kitty to snap off a stick from one of the shrubs. One thing I'd learned in my short time inside the Hockomock: if the land didn't support something big and green, the land didn't support at all.

A yell echoed through the trees. It wasn't a scream of terror, but my name followed by Kitty's. We'd lost Cody but found Dell.

Kitty climbed a nearby rock, standing on it so she could better see the wood line behind us. She yelled out, her voice cracking halfway through. The next thing we heard was Jess's voice calling back to us. My phone buzzed a second later.

Hold still we're coming.

What if Mary's looking for us? I texted back.

Dell can get us out quick.

I joined Kitty on the rock to wait. Crunching underbrush, rustling leaves—even expecting Dell and Jess, I prepared for the worst, the stick in my hand ready for Mary. When Jess's bandaged head popped out from behind a tree, I relaxed, but I never let my eyes stop skimming the landscape. I wouldn't be surprised again.

Dell followed behind Jess, her cane replaced by a piece of wet, moldy wood that looked like a broken fence slat. Her tank top was shredded over her stomach with a nasty rake of claw marks.

"Where's Cody?" she asked. Kitty and I stayed silent, though I did point in the direction of the sandpit. Dell sucked in a breath. "She's gone? Where's Mary?"

"Cody dragged Mary into the sand," I said. "She told us to leave her. They sank."

"Oh. Oh, my." Dell's jaw quivered like she might cry, too. "I'm so sorry."

I shrugged, not sure of what to say. "Are you okay?" I gestured at her middle, hoping it wasn't another Cody-scale wound.

"I'll be fine. Surface cuts only."

"It should have been you, Jess. You did this and it should have been you." Kitty's voice started off soft but grew louder by the word. Her eyes were swollen from crying, her nose red and crusted with snot. "It's your fault. IT SHOULD HAVE BEEN YOU."

Jess dropped her gaze to the soiled tips of our shoes, her nod so slight I barely caught it. "I'm sorry."

"Sorry?" Kitty snorted like a bull before the red cape. "Sorry doesn't cover it. Two people are dead. We should throw you in the pit with Mary so she won't come after the rest of us."

Jess flinched. "I never meant for any of it to happen."

It was the wrong thing to say. Kitty screamed in Jess's face—no words, just ear-punishing bellows that blasted out one after the other.

I clapped my hands over my ears. Kitty didn't stop until Jess stepped toward her. Immediately, I put myself between them, a human shield. I didn't know what Jess intended, and I didn't trust her enough to find out. Dell grabbed Jess's shoulder and yanked her back.

"Stop, Jessica." Jess tried to shake her off, but Dell held tight. "I said stop."

Jess stopped.

"I want to leave here. I hate this. I hate everything," Kitty screamed.

"Then let's get you out. Give me a moment." Dell retrieved her phone from the fanny pack. "I'll call the sheriff to get Co—" She paused to suck in a breath. "To get the situation taken care of. We'll see how he wants to progress with you talking to Elsa."

"Fine." Kitty jerked her head away so she wouldn't have to look at any of us. I glowered at Jess, the three feet between us stretching miles.

Dell led us through the swamp, droning on as she talked to the sheriff. I shivered despite the heat and humidity. A bird flew by to perch in the closest tree. I tuned in to the rest of the birds then, the tweets boisterous and cheery from the swamp around me. They'd been so still during Mary's attack; maybe their ruckus meant she was truly gone.

"I'm glad you're okay," Jess mumbled from behind me.

I couldn't say the same to her. "How'd you get away from Mary? She followed you guys first."

Jess's bark of laughter was harsh and humorless. "We found a patch of swamp gas and ran behind it. Hard to imagine, but even Mary has her limits."

If something could be evil enough to scare Bloody Mary Worth, I never wanted to see it for myself.

When Dell gave us directions to the sheriff's house, I typed them into my phone. I didn't trust myself to remember my name after all that happened, never mind an address.

"Jessica and I are staying here to meet the deputy," Dell said. "Sheriff Hawthorne is expecting you at Hawthorne House. It's the oldest building in town. They don't offer tours anymore, not since Karen went away, but . . . well. He's offered a meal and hot showers."

We were supposed to stay with Cody. . . .

I had to swallow a whimper.

"Why do we have to go see him? Can't he just take us to Elsa?" Kitty asked.

"His wife is involved. He wants to make sure you won't upset her. Karen and Elsa have been roommates since they entered the hospital. When one moved to assisted living, the other followed." Dell cleared her throat, her hand pressing over her scraped middle. I had a feeling there was information she didn't want to share. Jess and she had more things in common than their blood.

"Okay, but can we trust him? He's a Hawthorne," Kitty pressed.

Dell nodded. "Yes. I do, anyway. He understands our plight. Jonas has weights of his own that make him cooperative."

I tried not to roll my eyes. I couldn't imagine anyone having a weight like Mary.

Kitty slid from her rock to tap my elbow. "Fine. Let's go."

"Where are you girls staying again?" Dell called after us.

"Cody's," I decided on the spot without consulting Kitty. Maybe there was something in Cody's stash that would help. Dell estimated a twenty-minute walk from where we were to the road, but we halved it; as soon as we escaped the Worth women, we jogged, only pausing once for Kitty to catch her breath. We never said a word. I climbed into the SUV exhausted, miserable, and scared. And then I saw the Home Depot bags in the backseat.

Cody. I'm sorry.

Grief and self-loathing bubbled up inside of me.

I could have done more.

Kitty reached out to squeeze my knee, the first she'd acknowledged me since we left the others.

"Text your mom to tell her you're okay. It'll make you feel better." I didn't know about that, but I grabbed my phone and sent a message. It wasn't much more than telling Mom I loved her and I'd talk to her the next day, but in some small way it did make things a little bit easier. Well, that and the small hope that maybe Mary had been sunk for good.

Kitty grabbed the GPS from the glove compartment and set it up on the dashboard. I peered down the SUV's hood at the crisscrossing rusty chains and the NO TRESPASSING sign at the entrance to the swamp. Every time the wind rustled the trees, I flinched. And when Kitty drove away from the Hockomock, I prayed I'd never have to set foot in it again.

17

"Did Cody ever talk about her family?" Kitty turned the car onto a back road with faded paint lines and overgrown grass poking up through cracks in the sidewalk. Every third house was boarded up, the two intact houses between wearing their age in the peeling roofs and weatherworn shingles.

I glanced at Dell's directions. "I know she has some, but she never talked about it. She was really private. Keep going straight."

We passed a diner called Flo's Joe, an abandoned vegetable stand, and a gas station with an old rusted-out car on concrete blocks out front. The GPS beeped, and Kitty turned onto a curvy dirt road with no streetlights.

"You'll miss her," Kitty said quietly.

I looked out the window. "Yeah, I will. She helped me a lot. If I'd kept her out of this, maybe she'd—"

"Don't, Shauna." Kitty patted my arm. "Cody made that choice. It sucks and I won't ever forget that or her, but she made that choice. Don't shoulder that. It's not fair to yourself."

A lot of things aren't fair, but that doesn't make them less true.

⁣   ◦◦◦

Hawthorne House wasn't what I expected. I'd pictured an immaculate home with expensive cars parked out front. Instead, it was a sprawling, run-down manor house long past its glory days. Barren, unattended fields bordered the twisting driveway. The fences were collapsed, half of the connecting posts snapped off or rotting. It was separated from its closest neighbor by miles.

Oddly, one field on the right was in perfect condition. No weeds, no plants. The soil looked freshly tilled, and the fence was perfectly maintained. Emerald grass lined the outside perimeter, contrasting starkly with the dirt drive and the yellow crabgrass carpeting the rest of the property.

Kitty parked opposite the front door of the main house. At least I thought it was the main house—it was hard to tell. Hawthorne House was two separate houses connected by an enormous barn. The one on the left looked lived-in—the screen door was propped, the windows open to let the breeze pass through. The shingles were gray with age, but someone had taken the time to replace the ones near the eaves. A fresh coat of paint covered the black shutters. A hanging fuchsia added a splash of brilliant pink to the wraparound porch.

The house on the right was almost identical to the one on

the left, except it looked like the set of a horror movie. Boards covered the windows, slatted so efficiently from top to bottom I couldn't tell the condition of the glass underneath. The front door was equally inaccessible; iron hoops nailed to the house front allowed chains to crisscross the entryway, a padlock tethering them together near the ground.

The only thing intact was the cupola and widow's walk on the roof. It was a large square—twelve by twelve—each wall constructed of three floor-to-ceiling windows abutting one another. A black, pointed roof cast shadows on the upper panes of glass. A narrow white door the same size as one of the windows faced the chimney flute. The paint was in good shape, and the fence rail stood tall despite missing half its rungs.

I glanced back at the first house. No cupola. It was only present on this house. It looked like the two roofs should have been swapped so that the cupola could join the lived-in part of the house, it was that well preserved.

"I wish this was the worst place I'd been all day," Kitty said.

"Agreed." I climbed from the SUV, reeking like a sewer. Kitty shared my concern. She sniffed her sweatshirt before pulling it off and tossing it into the truck. Dell said the sheriff offered showers. I hoped that was still the case.

Thunderous stomps inside the house called my attention to the screen door. I half expected Godzilla to emerge, but Sheriff Hawthorne was average height and average weight with what my mother would call "ruddy skin." His dark brown hair was streaked with silver at his temples, his mustache and heavy brows sporting a similar salt-and-pepper effect. He wore fawn-colored steel-toed work boots, accounting for his heavy tread. Camouflage pants and a faded gray T-shirt with a charity picnic logo printed across the chest completed the outfit.

"Kitty and Shauna?" he asked, his voice deep.

I nodded. "She's Kitty, I'm Shauna. Thank you for seeing us."

"I do what I can. LYDIA. BRAN. COME OUT HERE." The last was aimed at the house. A childish squeal preceded a little boy shoving his way outside. He had the same green eyes and dark hair as his father, though his skin was honeyed brown. He wore a Batman T-shirt and blue jeans with dirty knees.

The teenaged girl shared the boy's skin tone, but her features were softer: almond-shaped eyes, full lips, a lovely nose sprinkled with freckles. Her sundress was yellow with two big pockets along the front, and her feet were bare. She slid in behind her father, her hand extending to rest on the little boy's back. The sheriff didn't like her shyness; he *tsk*ed and drew her forward by the elbow. She looked down at the ground in response.

"Lydia's your age. Bran's seven," the sheriff said.

I waved. Kitty managed a "Nice to meet you."

"I'm sorry about your friend," the sheriff said, his hand skimming over Bran's dark head. "Officer Stone will contact Miss Jackson's family, if she has any."

He glanced at his daughter. "Food's cooking?" Lydia nodded. Bran tried to squirm from her grasp, but she held tight, her hands clasping on his shoulders.

"Can I watch *Teen Titans*?" Bran asked.

The sheriff eyeballed him. "Be polite, Bran."

"Okay. Nice to meet you, Shaunakitty. Now can I go watch *Teen Titans*?" He said our names so fast, they were indiscernible.

The sheriff sighed and shooed him off. "My son the whirl-wind." Sheriff Hawthorne forced a smile, but it was out of place on his face—strained and unnatural, as if he wasn't sure how smiles were supposed to work. "How long on dinner, Lydia?"

"A half hour, probably," the girl said. She had one of those soft, low voices that under better circumstances I would have wanted to listen to for a while, but I was too sore and smelly and miserable to enjoy anything.

"Good. You girls are welcome to stay, but I have two rules if you do." He looked between us so we could see the serious-ness on his face. "One, no saying the word G-H-O-S-T in front of Bran. He gets nightmares. Speak in code. Second, and by far the most important." He pointed past my shoulder toward the one good field among all the decrepit ones. "You don't go there. Under any circumstance." He leveled a heavy stare on us. It was hard to tell if this was a request, a warning, or a threat.

I nodded slowly and could see Kitty doing the same from the corner of my eye. The sheriff instantly relaxed.

"We understand each other, then. Go clean up before dinner. We'll talk about Elsa once you're fed."

∽

"What's with the field?" Kitty whispered to me as we dressed in the spare room. "Is it, like, murder field?"

I looked out the window to the front yard, gazing at the near-black dirt and tidy fence. "No idea, but something's not right."

"No, it's not." Kitty raked a comb through her hair and headed for the bedroom door. She glanced at me over her shoulder. "Maybe everyone in this stupid town has their own monster."

We went downstairs to join the Hawthornes at the dinner table. Lydia had made roasted chicken for dinner with mashed potatoes. I wondered how she knew how to cook when all I could do was microwave popcorn, but then I remembered that her mother had been in the hospital for a long time. Lydia probably had to grow up fast.

"How much do you know about Mary?" I asked the sheriff, my fork dragging tracks through my potatoes.

The sheriff eyed Bran, who was cramming broccoli into his mouth. "Enough that you don't need to go into detail, and likely shouldn't because of present company." He paused. "What were you hoping to get from Elsa? She and Karen—my wife—share a room at the facility. They've been roommates for almost seven years."

I did the math. Karen had been institutionalized near Bran's birth. A fact that seemed noteworthy.

"We want to ask what happened with Mary. We know lots of things that seem important, but we don't know how they connect. If we can piece together the whole story, maybe we can figure out how to stop her." I paused to take a bite of food. "Hannah Worth didn't drown. We know the pastor quickly married Elizabeth Hawthorne after Mary and Hannah died. Why? And what does it have to do with what is happening now?"

The sheriff and Lydia exchanged a look. The sheriff motioned at me with his fork. "After supper, Lydia can take you out to the family plot."

Kitty looked up from her dinner. "It's here?"

"This is the original Hawthorne House. Or, well..." The sheriff pulled a biscuit in half and crammed one side in his mouth. "It's the replacement building from the mid-seventeen hundreds. The original burnt down with our ancestor and his family inside. But everyone since then is buried in a private cemetery in the back, including Elizabeth and Starkcrowe. Family previous to the fire is buried at the center of town, at First Church."

"Starkcrowe's not really buried here. It's just a plot," Lydia said quietly. She looked from her father to us. "The family put up a marker, but there's no one buried below."

The sheriff grunted. "Yes. An empty plot. Starkcrowe ran off shortly after the marriage. Elizabeth's father had him proclaimed dead after six months. Judges could do that sort of thing."

I filed that away. Starkcrowe had a history of bad behavior, yes, but he was a pastor. Running off on his wife would have been scandalous. And what of Elizabeth?

"I'd like to go," Kitty answered. When I cast her a side-eyed glance, she shrugged. "I'm curious."

I wasn't interested in the graveyard, but I'd go because Kitty was going.

Dinner descended into quiet—the sheriff was not the chatty type, his daughter no more inclined to speak than he was. Occasionally, I'd catch her peering at me, and she'd smile, but then quickly turn her attention to her younger brother. Bran writhed to get out of his seat halfway through the meal, but she kept him quiet with promises of cartoons and dessert. After he finished his vegetables, she let him run off to watch TV in the other room.

The moment he was gone, the sheriff got conversational again. He lowered his voice so it wouldn't carry. "I understand what you girls are up against, and I'll do what I can to help, but my concern is Karen. If you upset Elsa, you upset my wife. They rely on one another. I understand this is a difficult situation, but if you promise to keep your questioning delicate and leave when it's time to leave, I'll make the call."

"We'll be careful," Kitty swore. The sheriff looked to me for separate confirmation.

"We're not out to upset anyone. Thank you, Sheriff."

"Let me set it up, then." He got up from the table and wandered off to use the phone. His daughter stood, headed down the hall, and disappeared from view.

"Strange," whispered Kitty. I shrugged. Not as strange as everything else we'd seen in Solomon's Folly.

I cleared the table out of habit. It was my chore at home, and I tended to jump to it at other houses, too. As I scraped plates into the garbage, I remembered Mrs. McAllister giving Jess grief because I helped out and Jess didn't. It made me sad to think about—I'd probably never be at the McAllister dinner table again.

Especially if Mary catches Jess.

But that would mean Mary crawled out of the quicksand.

That was impossible, wasn't it?

If it's so impossible, why are we still searching for answers?

I gritted my teeth and stacked the plates into a neat pile. I was about to carry them to the sink when Lydia returned from the kitchen. Seeing me, she gasped and rushed over, taking the plates away and putting them back on the table.

"No, no. Don't worry about—I have it. Thank you, though. You wanted to see the family plot, yes?" Her smile was too bright as she ushered me away. I had no idea what I'd done, but it was clear something was wrong.

"Did I offend you?" I asked, not sure if I should apologize.

"Not at all." That was all Lydia said, pausing by the screen door to slip into a pair of sandals. Kitty joined us outside, falling into step beside me past the cars, the barn, and the dilapidated half of Hawthorne House.

"Why are there two houses?" My eyes followed dried vines of dead ivy as they wound around the pillars supporting the porch overhang.

"At one time there were twins in the family and they didn't want to fight over the house, so they built an addition that mirrored the original construction. The run-down side is the original building, though my great-grandfather abandoned it in the fifties when it got too hard to repair. The part we live in was built about a hundred years later and is still serviceable."

She guided us toward the woods along the property edge, a path lined with white painted stones veering off into the unknown. Lydia headed straight for it, but I turned to get a different view of the older house. An attached room on the back looked different than the rest of the house—a pile of twisted metal that made me think of a mangled jungle gym. Most of it was rectangular, maybe fifteen feet long and ten feet wide, but the top portion was domed.

"What's that?"

"That used to be a conservatory," she said.

I edged closer to check it out. The floor of the conservatory was cracked concrete, dead stems poking up through the fissures. The broken remnants of a stone fountain aligned with the apex of the dome. Abandoned pots and planters littered the shelves and ground, dirt scattered everywhere. Ivy wound around the outside frame and climbed toward the roof, some of it brown, some of it green. I followed the green all the way to the widow's walk.

There was a stained glass window on the back of the cupola. Two regular windows flanked it, as tall as the cupola itself and rectangular, but the middle window was domed-top stained glass. The glass was dark thanks to a thick layer of dust on the inside, but the design was still visible. It was a bird in flight, its wings back, its beak pointed down. The metal shaping the picture was weather-beaten and silvery.

I pointed up at it. "What's that?"

Kitty followed my gaze and frowned. "It looks like something you'd see on a tombstone."

"Yes." Lydia motioned at the white stone path. Kitty and I followed her into the woods. Past a line of trees and down a series of wide stone steps, there was a grassy clearing with lines of tombstones arranged in neat rows. The front stones weren't arranged as evenly, but they were the oldest—the earlier Hawthornes probably had no idea that their family line would roost there for the next three centuries.

"Like I said, the oldest Hawthornes are buried outside of the First Church at the center of town." Lydia drifted through the rows, looking at the dates. It was easy-ish to find people, because they were buried in the order that they died. Rows two through four were all the eighteen hundreds.

"The bird," Kitty said. "It's on all of the markers. Look." She broke away from me to approach the nearest tombstone. It was shaped like a cross with an ornate circle at the top. Inside of that circle was the same crow we'd seen in the stained glass window.

"It's a family crest," Lydia said. "It's been our marker for as long as there's been Hawthornes in Solomon's Folly."

Kitty ran her fingers over the carving. "Usually you see doves on tombstones, not crows. . . ."

Lydia hesitated before answering, as if she had to calculate what she said. "Crows are survivors. They always get what they think they want."

"What they think they want?" Kitty asked the question before I could. "Not what they want?"

"Yes." Lydia paused in front of a simple square stone, bleached white by time. The crow was carved at the top of this stone, too, its claws clasping a broken bud. "Here."

I looked down.

ELIZABETH JANE HAWTHORNE JENSON
AUGUST 31, 1846–MAY 16, 1869
BELOVED WIFE AND DAUGHTER

Next to it was a much smaller stone, simple by comparison and lacking the bird etching.

PHILIP ELIJAH STARKCROWE III
OCTOBER 5, 1839–APRIL 8, 1865
SERVANT OF GOD

"They both died young," I said. "Elizabeth remarried? To a Jenson?"

Lydia nodded. "He's not buried here. Their marriage didn't last long, as you can see. He must be interred at First Church. That's where most of old Folly is buried."

I tried to put the dates in order; Mary died six months before Philip disappeared. Elizabeth died four years after that. That wasn't much time, and for a moment I wondered if Mary had anything to do with it. I crouched before Elizabeth's tombstone, my legs tight and sore from running earlier. "Starkcrowe ran off, but how did Elizabeth die?"

Lydia cleared her throat like she was embarrassed. "I want to give you something." She reached into the pocket of her dress and produced a folded letter. "Don't tell my father. He's funny about family things, but I—I don't know if the letter will help, but I'd rather you see it than not. We all have our problems. Ours is ... well, strange things happen here, too, in the field.

I don't know much about your Mary, but I can sympathize. A little."

"What *is* going on with the field?" Kitty asked.

Lydia's cheeks stained red. "Nothing you have to worry about if you don't go into it. Just be careful in The Folly. Its secrets are old and ugly and dangerous." She thrust the letter at me, desperate to change the subject. "I thought you might want to see this. It might be relevant. I don't know if anyone told you, but Elizabeth Hawthorne hanged herself."

November 23, 1864

Lizzie,

There is a marked difference between what I cannot do and what I will not do. One suggests inability. The other suggests refusal to change a prior course of action. In regards to your engagement, I am of the latter category, which is how I shall remain. This is not a negotiation. You will wed Philip Starkcrowe in two weeks' time.

It would perhaps be simpler for me to explain in person, but I cannot shirk my responsibilities to the state of Massachusetts. As you are a devoted daughter of the House of Hawthorne, you will do your duty without further complaint. Anything else would prove your mother right, and she is harpy enough without that fuel.

I know you see this as a great injustice, but from my perspective, it is an instance of cause reaping effect. While the recent unpleasantness was handled, it was not without its complications, and the expediency of certain deeds requires me to make plans I would not have made elsewise. Your marriage is one such example. I dislike having this stain under my crest. It befouls my house. I will, in due time, see to its removal, but until then a marriage guarantees the agreeability of all involved parties.

As for the rest of your concerns, I will address them because I love you best, but I have little patience for inane female blather.

The Adderly boy was never an acceptable match. Your idiot dog is smarter, and I'm fairly convinced my boots could outsmart the dog, so what does that say for the oaf? I would not pair Hawthorne blood with Adderly blood any more than I would pair a champion stallion with the lowliest swine. I told you years ago this was not a realistic expectation, and I reiterate it now. Move past these fanciful notions and understand that Adderly is barely fit to polish your shoes, never mind be on your arm.

I hope I have made myself perfectly clear.

Mr. Starkcrowe is a pastor and devoted to God. Once he is married, I have no doubt he will be committed to you if for no other reason than fear for his immortal soul. He shares ideology with Jonathan Edwards (perhaps you should reread "Sinners in the Hands of an Angry God"). Philandering defies a very basic tenet. There, too, is the matter of his flaxen fixation leaping to her death in a river. I do not know how to explain to you that being jealous of a dead woman is ridiculous.

I recognize that he has a temper, Elizabeth, but I have faith you will comport yourself with dignity and decorum as befits a pastor's wife. He will have less reason to anger if you curb your barbed tongue. Should he prove excessive with his disciplines, I will speak to him, but I will not borrow a problem that does not yet exist.

Lastly, your claims that I have forsaken you are hysterical, insulting, and patently false. You dropped inclement weather upon my doorstep, and like most inclement weather, I batten down the hatches until the storm passes. I do not "sacrifice you" to Starkcrowe as you so put it. I clean up the mess you have made with the tools at my disposal. It is my duty to see that the

Hawthorne name perseveres. Without us, Solomon's Folly falls to ruin. I will not have that on my conscience.

Whatever is on your conscience is your own doing. Perhaps next time you will exercise more caution in your affairs.

Your Loving Father,

Seymour

18

We climbed into Kitty's car armed with the sheriff's cell phone number, a nine o'clock appointment for the next morning at the Geraldine Hawthorne Assisted Living Community, and the stashed letter.

Lydia dashed into the house after a hasty good-bye while Sheriff Hawthorne stood on the porch, his arms crossed over his chest. He glanced at his watch. "I have an appointment at quarter of eight tonight, but I'll be back at half past. Are you sure you don't want to stay here? It might be uncomfortable at the Jackson house, all things considered."

"We need to look around Cody's house to see if there's anything that will help with Mary," I said. "She told us how to get in." Any hope I had that Mary sunk into the quicksand for good was overshadowed by the fear that she was still out there.

The sheriff eyed me. "You can look and then come back here. I'll be up until midnight, but call anytime."

"He's a cop, Shauna," Kitty said. "We might be safer. Plus he's a Hawthorne, which might deter Mary, if she got out of the swamp."

Or maybe she'd come looking for revenge against the Hawthorne family.

The sheriff stepped off the porch and leaned into Kitty's open car window. "I can't do a lot to help you girls. I know..." He paused. "Being sheriff in a town like this, I know things. Things that shouldn't be possible but are. I'm limited because of my responsibilities. My wife. My kids. The town. The town needs the Hawthornes more than the Hawthornes need the town. We're tied here for better or worse."

Without us, Solomon's Folly falls to ruin. I will not have that on my conscience, Seymour Hawthorne wrote in his letter. One hundred fifty years later, his great-times-many grandson was still saying the same thing.

"The point is," the sheriff continued, "I can't help you beat this thing, but I can give you beds and food while you do. I'd be happy to have one less nightmare on my conscience."

"We'll be back," Kitty answered for both of us. She cast me a guilty look. "I know you want to stay at Cody's, but it feels wrong without her. Looking around is fine, but sleeping there—no. Please."

I sighed. Of the three options—Hawthorne House, Dell's, or Cody's—it was the best of a bad lot. "Thanks, Sheriff Hawthorne." I said. "I'll text you before we come back."

∞

The sun was setting by the time we pulled into Cody's driveway. I expected to hear the crickets heralding the dusk, but it was silent. In summer in Bridgewater, the kids played in the streets until dark. Solomon's Folly was different. Parents tucked their kids away before suppertime.

Looking at Cody's gray house, my chest grew tight. I climbed from the SUV to walk around to the backyard. I'd never been behind the house, and seeing the overflowing trash barrels, the old furniture stacked and ready to go to the dump, I understood why. It was an obstacle course of junk.

At least there was a path to the concrete steps. I lifted the dingy mat and found a key where Cody had left it. Kitty picked her way around the mess to join me as I pushed open the back door. It led straight into the kitchen. The house was in much better shape than I remembered. Flypapers no longer covered the ceiling. The furniture wasn't new, but it was new to Cody. The fake leather couches in the living room replaced the threadbare stuff from the last visit. She'd tidied the house as well—the floors were swept, the curtains washed. A fresh coat of paint brightened the living room and hallway.

She thought she had things to live for. She thought she had more time.

Kitty closed the door behind us. I made my way to the living room. I'd been to the house only once, but I remembered the shelves stacked with books and papers. They were sorted now—another thing Cody had cleaned once she was freed from Mary's curse. I tried not to think about it too much as I grabbed the photo albums and manila envelopes from the bottom shelf.

I'd gone through the pictures before, but Cody hadn't shared the rest.

The first envelope was full of newspaper clippings about missing girls. The stories of their disappearances were similar to Anna's—teenagers gone without a trace. I wondered about the missing girls' friends: how many of them lived with this same burden? Knowing what happened and not being able to talk about it? How many were chalked up as runaways when the reality was much worse—Mary had taken them and used them to fuel her own decaying body.

That's how she got the fresh fingers.

I shuddered, handing the clippings to Kitty, but she waved me off. She sat on the couch, her cell phone in her hands, thumbs flying.

"Bronx?" I asked, sorting piles.

"Yes. He wants me to text him every night. He's worried about me." She sniffled, wiping her runny nose across the back of her arm.

Which reminded me, I needed to text Mom. In a little while.

Kitty continued. "He's mad at me."

"Why?" I pulled an envelope from inside the bigger envelope and wondered if there'd be a third envelope in the second one, like Russian nesting dolls with paper. Instead, there were six paper-clipped pages, the top one a photocopy of a photo.

"Because I told him wh-what to do with my stuff if I died."

I jabbed her in the knee with my thumb. "Hey, now. I won't let anything happen to you."

"I'm not sure that's up to you so much as Mary."

"Enough, Kitty," I snapped, rougher than I intended. Mary wouldn't take another friend from me. I wouldn't let her.

The picture on top was of Elizabeth Hawthorne standing with three girls her age, all of them wearing dark, button-up dresses with belled skirts and lace collars. Elizabeth wore a decorative shawl around her shoulders. The girls clasped hands, telegraphing affection, but their spines were stiff, their smiles lukewarm. I'd read that old cameras had slow exposure times so people had to maintain their poses for a long period. If the toothy smile faltered midtake, it'd screw up the picture.

Cody had written on the page with a red marker—arrows pointing at each of the girls. The short, slight girl with the curly dark hair on the left was Sarah Ashby. She held hands with Elizabeth, who held hands with a tall, heavyset girl named Meredith Richards. The last girl on the right was pretty and of average size, the only blonde of the group. Her name was Agnes Willowcroft. They stood in front of a fencepost, but in the far back I recognized Hawthorne House—I knew it was the older side from the widow's walk.

I flipped to the next page, a photocopy of an official death certificate from the town of Solomon's Folly. The next three pages were also death certificates. The strange thing was, they were incomplete. The names were filled in, the dates of death, but the causes were left blank except for Elizabeth's, which listed cerebral hypoxia.

Sarah Ashby was born on June 2, 1847, and died April 30, 1865.

Meredith Richards was born on November 3, 1847, and died June 19, 1865.

Agnes Willowcroft was born February 6, 1845, and died August 4, 1865.

Elizabeth died four whole years later.

"Mary did it," I said, skimming through them. "She killed them. The other girls, I bet."

Kitty put the phone aside to reach for my papers. I handed them over, pointing at the empty fields. "Why else would the doctor leave them blank? You can't put *ghost* down as a reason."

Kitty surveyed the dates. "I wonder if that's why Elizabeth killed herself. All her friends were dead."

"Or guilt, maybe. That letter from earlier." I pulled out Seymour's letter, careful with the vellum. Unlike the others we'd read, it was an original from the nineteenth century. It was in excellent shape, but with a family history as huge as the Hawthornes, I wasn't surprised they'd kept it in good condition. They had a legacy to preserve.

I folded out the letter on the end table next to the couch. "Elizabeth's father was such a jerk. But notice how he keeps talking about the bad stuff Elizabeth brought back to him to handle? This is right after Mary died. He's talking in code. Like, right here. 'While the recent unpleasantness was handled, it was not without its complications, and the expediency of certain deeds requires me to make plans I would not have made elsewhere.' He's talking about Mary. He has to be."

Kitty stopped to reread the letter. Finishing, she blinked at me over the top of the yellowing page. "What if Elizabeth killed Mary? All this time, we said it was Starkcrowe because he was mean to Mary, but what if Elizabeth did it?"

19

There was weight being in a person's house hours after she died. It was life put on pause, the living intending to return to her nest but denied the chance. A loaf of bread with the bag open at one end. Unwashed dishes piled in the sink. A half-filled garbage bag by the door. Toilet cleaner left in the toilet for a later scrubbing.

Signs of Cody's reclusion remained. Torn pieces of dark paper that used to cover the windows were stacked by the front door. The pictures were stuck to the wall with gum, none of them framed. Flypaper hung in the corner of the living room, curled and peppered with bug carcasses.

My unease matched my sadness.

We sifted through Cody's collection, though most of the things we'd already seen. There were some pictures of missing girls, and a map marked where disappearances occurred, but none of it helped solve Mary's death.

I swept the other rooms, trying not to miss anything. Two bedrooms with double beds, dressers, and bookshelves. A bathroom with no vanity. A small office with stacks of unopened notebooks, a transistor radio, and piles of books. There was no computer, nor were there screens, monitors, or mirrors of any type.

"I don't want to root around in her drawers," Kitty said. "That makes me feel bad to think about."

There were merits to thoroughness, though—what if Cody forgot to share something important? She told us a lot of things over the previous months. Something could have escaped her mind.

We could be looking all night for a needle in a haystack. Cody deserves some privacy.

"Okay. I'll grab what we have and we can go."

I shut off the lights and closed the doors behind me. Kitty waited for me in the living room while I finished up packing. I decided to take the paperwork but leave Cody's personal albums in case her family wanted the photos. As I stuffed them back into the bookshelf, a shrill wail echoed outside the house. I froze. It wasn't the same pitch as Mary, but it was much too close.

It can't be. No, it's not. So what is it?

It happened again, an exaggerated groan that sounded less like fury and more like despair. It was joined by a second and third voice, like a pack of wolves, but that wasn't quite right either. They were too human sounding. Frantic whispers followed the baying, the voices talking over one another more than to each other in a tongue I didn't understand.

I glanced at Kitty. The color had drained from her face. "What?"

She said nothing, only pointed at the side window. Fog. Dense and green and swirling in a series of tiny maelstroms. It reminded me of the fog in Mary's mirror, only softer and wispier along the edges. It curled around the house, tendrils licking at the front window and creeping skyward before dissipating into the ether.

"What is that?" Kitty demanded, but she knew. We both knew.

Ghost fog. Here.

Another unholy chorus of whispers and groans echoed through the living room from the window. I stood still, my eyes wide, my pulse pounding in my ears. The fog drifted away, toward the other side of the property, the thickest parts of it rolling and roiling like a nest of ghost serpents.

"Now. Go now." Kitty took off at a hard run through the kitchen door. I followed, shoving the house key under the welcome mat. Night had fallen, the sky black and empty of stars. The slam of Cody's door seemed to beckon the fog back; I could hear the whispers swinging back around the side lawn.

We sprinted for the car. Kitty shoved the key into the ignition and tore away from the neighborhood with a squeal of tires. A haunting screech followed us, the ghost fog an amorphous blob of fury sweeping back and forth across the pavement. Unlike Mary, it moved slowly.

"WHAT IS THIS?" Kitty slapped at the dashboard and shrieked. "What's going on?"

We sped to the sheriff's house. The two traffic stops were torturous thanks to the creaking woods surrounding us. I scanned the trees expecting green fog to spill out from the brush. Nothing, though the distant groaning turned to shrill, high-pitched wails and yips. Halfway to the Hawthorne farm, gray fog crept in from the marshes and rose to swallow the car, just as dense and swirling as the ghostly stuff we'd left behind. It reminded me of cauldron smoke.

"No green," I said. "It's normal fog."

"That doesn't make it easy to drive through." Kitty's hands gripped ten and two on the wheel. We couldn't see more than three feet in front of us, the high beams only worsening the conditions.

"This is insane," Kitty murmured. "I hate this town."

More baying echoed from behind. I locked the doors, my fingers trembling as they pressed the button. We drove in silence, one terrible, terrifying question on my mind.

What the hell is wrong with Solomon's Folly?

The rain came as we settled into our bedroom at Hawthorne House. The room was dated, the rose wallpaper faded, the window curtains threadbare and yellow from age. The double bed had a metal headboard that looked institutional, like something out of an old hospital. When the rain started to pelt the windows with fierce slaps, Lydia scurried in to put a pan in the corner. She apologized for intruding, and darted down the hall to her own room.

I hadn't noticed the leak in the roof until the *ping ping ping* of raindrops striking the pan began. It distracted me at first, but as I jotted into my notebook all that we knew about Mary, I tuned it out.

"You texted your mom, right?" Kitty asked, the glow of the phone illuminating her face.

"Yes. She said good night."

Kitty put her phone aside to peer at me. "So if we find Mary's body, are we still going to burn it?"

I shrugged. "I guess? Fire works on everything else. I don't know why it wouldn't with this. I'm hoping that if we solve the murder, Mary will be at rest and we won't have to worry."

"Maybe we should ask Dell," Kitty said. "It'd be really stupid if we went through all of this to find the body and then didn't know what to do with it. I'm glad we're figuring out what happened with Elizabeth, but there's still a lot we don't know, like what's the connection to mirrors? I understand the thing about mirrors sucking out the souls of the dying, but that doesn't explain how Mary gets in water, chrome, plastic."

I studied my list. I had everything clustered according to topic—discoveries about the Worths in one column, the Hawthornes another, Starkcrowe a third. There was another short list for miscellaneous facts, like how Mary was summoned, where she could appear and under what conditions. "She pops up in anything reflective. It's impossible."

"What do you mean?"

I tapped the page. "When we first talked about the mirror soul thing, we thought Mary appeared only there. But she doesn't. She's in reflections." Kitty glanced at me, confused. I tried to explain. "Okay, like, where have we seen her?"

"Mirrors. Glass. Water."

"Right, so limiting our search to mirrors is ignoring the other stuff, which is silly. There are too many possibilities. Trying to find one specific mirror tied to Mary isn't feasible."

Kitty tousled her hair, leaving her bangs askew on top of her head. "I get it. All the more reason to ask Dell."

I grabbed my phone and texted Jess. I meant to earlier when we got sidetracked with the sheriff, Cody's, and the ghost fog.

Hey, you awake? I typed.

It took her a minute to respond. *Yeah.*

Now that I had her attention, I wasn't quite sure what to do with it. I glanced at Kitty. "Do you want to stop over Dell's house after we see Elsa? It's probably easier to ask Dell in person than to filter through Jess."

She frowned. "Fine. As long as it's quick. Seeing Jess turns my stomach."

"Okay. Not a problem." I got back to texting.

We're seeing Elsa at nine tomorrow. Can we stop by after? Need to talk to your aunt.

Sure was all she said.

I was about to put the phone aside when I asked one last question. *Any sign of Mary?*

No Mary or Cody. Sunk. Fishing out 2morrow cop said. Need tow truck.

I turned off the cell and slid it onto the end table. I didn't make the connection of why they'd want the tow truck immediately, but then I remembered the winch on the back. I rolled over on my side of the bed, my back facing Kitty.

"Night, Shauna." She turned off the light before rustling around beneath the blankets and going still. I wanted to fall asleep, but my emotions were too tangled. Fear of Mary. Fear of the fog. Sadness about Cody. Trepidation about meeting Elsa Samburg. I was a ball of bad feelings, and before I knew it, tears dribbled down my cheeks to soak the pillow below.

We're in over our heads, but we've come so far.

We've sacrificed so much.

Walking away was smart, but I couldn't do that to the woman who'd died today—who'd put her faith in me. Though Cody Jackson was weird and surly and occasionally crazier than a bat in a belfry, she'd been my friend, and I would miss her.

"Geraldine Hawthorne was my great-great-aunt," the sheriff explained over pancakes. The rain had stopped, though the skies were an abysmal gray. I had on my Windbreaker in case of a storm, my hair tied back because my curls frizzed in humidity. "She opened the facility to care for her elderly father. It started as a private hospital, but my father changed that in the seventies. It's been an assisted living complex ever since."

I ate my breakfast, sandwiched between Lydia and Kitty. Bran was off watching cartoons in the other room, his breakfast on a TV tray.

"I hope this isn't rude, but, like, didn't they meet at the institution?" Kitty fidgeted in her seat, clearly uncomfortable. "Sorry to be, you know. Sorry." She fumbled with it, but I wouldn't have done any better. It wasn't an easy topic.

The sheriff stabbed into his stack of pancakes a little more fiercely than necessary. "Yes. You do know that neither of them talk, yes? That's why they gravitated to one another to begin with. When I pushed to get Karen relocated, the doctors worried what the separation would do to them, so they sent Elsa with her. They live peacefully enough despite all their crazy."

Lydia flinched. "That word, Daddy. Please."

"Right. Sorry," he murmured. "I'm not as careful with my words as I should be sometimes." He concentrated on his breakfast, and again a meal with the Hawthornes turned oppressively quiet. Kitty nudged my foot with hers under the table. I returned the gesture.

I tried to help Lydia clean up breakfast, but she kept me away from the far side of the kitchen. It was a very specific area near the double windows she seemed intent to box off. Strange, because an earlier peek through the hall window revealed nothing but empty cornfields, an enormous weeping willow tree, a shed, and an overgrown apple orchard.

The sheriff wagged his fingers at Lydia, the pads blackened with what looked like mechanical grease. "I'll plan on you two for dinner. Or Lydia will. I'm working at noon and have to oversee the swamp dredge. I'll call Dell with what we find. Hopefully, there will be two bodies and you can put this thing behind you." He paused. "Not hopefully. That's the wrong—if you need something, you have my phone number."

He looked uncomfortable.

"Thanks," I said. "We're visiting Dell after Elsa, but I don't think there are any other plans. I really hope Elsa has some information she can share about Mary that we haven't found yet."

The sheriff nodded.

I stood from the table and headed outside, Kitty on my heels. As we approached the SUV, the sheriff called out, his hand holding open the screen door. His silhouette looked huge, his shoulders broad and filling the doorway. He stepped outside in his grease-smeared tank top, pressed uniform pants, and too-polished boots.

"Be careful with my wife. Elsa, too. Please. Both of them have been through too much. They don't need help being unhappy."

"I will, Sheriff. Thank you again for trusting us," I said.

20

The Geraldine Hawthorne facility was lovely in a colonial Americana way. The cadet-blue buildings had white shutters and tall white pillars supporting the roof overhangs. The pink and white gardens were meticulously pruned, the pathways to each building new red brick. The sheriff told us that Elsa and Karen were in Building Three and to ask for Nurse Lacy at the front desk.

"I wonder what happened to the sheriff's wife," Kitty mused as we walked through the guest parking lot. "I really want to know what's up in that field. Or maybe I don't. It'll make me more freaked-out about staying with him."

"I was just thinking the same thing. And I'm too chicken to outright ask him, so maybe this is one of those cases where ignorance is bliss." I glanced at my phone. Quarter to nine. We had plenty of time.

We passed a line of open windows in the first building, the music spilling out a fifties pop song. It was a seniors aerobics class, twenty or so grandmas and grandpas shuffling to the beat while a perky brunette instructor shouted instructions. One lady in the back row exercised while holding on to her walker. What she lacked in hand motions, she made up for with awkward bounces.

The next room was a seniors pottery class, the students no younger than sixty or seventy. Everywhere we looked, older people partook in group activities to start the day. Elsa and Karen weren't that old yet. To get them into a place like this, the sheriff probably had to pull some strings. The Hawthorne name probably helped.

My knees knocked as we approached Building Three. I wanted to question Elsa, but I couldn't forget that she was a trauma victim. I dreaded what would happen if I triggered her anxiety. We had too much at stake to lose the sheriff's support, and he wouldn't be pleased if I upset his wife. Kitty opened the door. A man with a long black ponytail smiled at us from behind a reception desk. He wore blue scrubs and a stethoscope that dangled from his neck like a python. "Can I help you?"

"Hi, I'm looking for Nurse Lacy?" I said.

"You're speaking to him."

I stared at him stupidly, not registering that a nurse could be a guy. He laughed, his face breaking into so many lines, it was as if he'd aged twenty years in a second.

"I get that a lot. Shauna and Kitty, right?" When I nodded,

he produced two lanyards with laminated passes and a clip-board. "Sign here and I'll take you down." Checked in, we fol-lowed Nurse Lacy from the desk and through a reception room, passing stairs, an elevator, and an empty community room with Ping-Pong tables and soda machines. "A couple of rules before you go in. No mirrors of any kind. No compacts, no nothing. Do you have any birds on you?"

"Wait, what?" Kitty asked, clearly confused.

Nurse Lacy chuckled. "I meant on your clothes. If so we'll get you a sweater. Elsa obsesses over birds, and if you want a decent interaction with her, we need to keep her restricted to the birds she already has, not ones she might want to collect."

Lacy continued. "Don't touch Karen, or Elsa will get upset. Don't be alarmed that Karen doesn't acknowledge you. That's typical behavior." He stopped outside of a closed door and smiled, his hand poised on the knob. "I doubt that you would, but please don't remove any of the contact paper on the windows. It's there for Elsa's benefit. If you have any questions, press the green button for the intercom. If there's an emergency, press the red button and I'll come."

He opened the door and motioned us in. I stopped before crossing the threshold.

"She can't speak, but can she write?" I whispered. I figured if Elsa couldn't tell us what happened with Mary, maybe she could write it down.

Nurse Lacy shook his head. "She has nerve damage from her injuries. If you absolutely need it, I can make another appointment when a doctor's in attendance, but she gets frustrated when her motor functions don't perform well."

"Oh. Okay. Thanks."

"No problem." He winked at me and poked his head inside. "Elsa, Karen. Your guests are here."

I walked in. It was an open floor plan apartment. The first room was a combination living room and kitchen, the kitchen immediately to my left, the living room extending all the way back to a wall of windows. Everything was Easter egg–colored. The wainscoting on the wall, pale yellow. The floral wallpaper above, yellow and pink flowers with mint green leaves. The couches were peach; the cabinets in the kitchen, robin's egg blue.

I understood what Nurse Lacy meant about the contact paper then. Instead of regular panes of glass, they'd taken the time to apply a clear plastic overcoat like you might see in a bathroom window for privacy. It was wavy and bubbly and allowed colors in but no definitive shapes.

Mary in the textured glass of the shower door, looking in at me, watchful but unable to pass through. This is the same. Elsa's protecting herself all these years later.

I licked my lips, looking to the doors on the right. Three in a row, the first open and revealing a mirrorless bathroom with cotton candy–pink walls and seashell decorations. The next two were closed. Bedrooms, I guessed, though one of them could be a closet.

The women we'd come to see sat in front of the windows at a chess table. I recognized the lady on the left as Karen

Hawthorne. Her daughter resembled her—beautiful features, smooth dark skin. Her hair was buzzed short to her scalp, silver at the temples but otherwise black. She didn't look at us, nor did she look at the chessboard before her.

Elsa played chess for both of them, swiping pawns from the board with glee, her face brightening with every play. She was short and round—Rubenesque, my mother would have said—with a tan that suggested she spent a lot of time outside. Her hair was auburn and cut short beneath her ears, the sides pulled up in silver barrettes. Her dress was a short-sleeved muumuu with bright purple flowers and lace at the neck.

When she turned to look at us, I was surprised by her youthfulness. Elsa had to be midforties, but the woman didn't have a wrinkle on her face.

She didn't acknowledge Kitty or me at first, instead glancing back at the board, but then she swooped up a queen, held it above her head like a prize, and stood. She walked our way, the queen outstretched before she put it in my hand, closing my fingers around it.

"She does that," Nurse Lacy whispered behind me. "Tries to give you things. There's a basket in the hall when you leave. I'll stay a few minutes to make sure things go smoothly."

I nodded and looked at the chess piece, then at Elsa. Her eyes were very blue, her nose a little too big, her mouth small. She wore stop sign–red lipstick.

Nurse Lacy hovered by the door. Elsa gestured at the couches in the living room, the two facing each other and separated by a wicker coffee table. There was no TV, though there was a stereo cabinet with the glass doors removed. On the wall, shelves upon shelves of bird figures made of clay, porcelain, and plush stared out at us. Parrots, pigeons, ducks—it seemed the type of bird mattered far less than the presence of feathers.

Elsa shooed us toward the couches and headed for the kitchen, the half wall allowing me to see her put a kettle on the stove. She lifted a tin of tea in one hand and coffee with the other.

"I'm set," Kitty said.

Elsa looked disappointed.

I didn't want to get off on the wrong foot. "I'd love tea, thank you." Elsa proceeded to assemble three cups despite Kitty declining. Elsa brought a steaming cup over to Karen, setting it on the table by her elbow. She touched Karen's hand, scowled, and retrieved a knitted blanket from one of the bedrooms, adjusting it around Karen's shoulders and kissing her cheek. Karen never stirred.

I watched Karen from the corner of my eye, curious to see if she blinked. It wasn't often, but it did happen. I wondered if she knew we were in the room.

Elsa returned to the kitchen, humming quietly as she put our cups on a tray. I'd been told Elsa was mute. It seemed she could make noise, she simply chose not to speak.

There was a soft click as Nurse Lacy let himself out of the room.

She delivered the tea to me, looming as I honeyed the brew and sipped.

"Thank you," I said. "It's great."

She grinned. I expected her to sit with us, but she whisked over to her birds, selecting four from the hundreds if not thousands of knickknacks. She presented her prizes in her right palm. Black birds, all of them. A wooden swan, a plastic crow, a windup pelican, and a stuffed vulture with a bright orange head. I smiled at her, and them, and she shoved them at me, indicating I should take them. I did, though she plucked the plushie from the pile and put it on my head, only to let it tumble down.

She pointed at herself, then at me, and did it again, the bird on my head released to fall to my lap.

"Is it a game?" Kitty asked.

Elsa sighed and shook her head, sitting with her tea. She lifted her hand and tapped above her heart. A fake hand. I hadn't noticed it when she'd bustled about, but now that she was still, I could see the metal joint at the wrist, silver against the flesh-colored prosthetic.

I wanted to ask. I needed to ask, but I was so afraid of setting her off. Mary's name was a powder keg ready to blow, so I went for a subtler approach. I pulled down the collar on my T-shirt, showing off the scars where Mary hooked me. It was weird, but Elsa understood. She reached out and brushed the air in front of my faded wounds like she wanted to touch them but didn't dare.

She nodded slowly and tapped her hand. Then she put the bird on top of my head and watched it plummet. I caught it before it struck the floor.

"We want to make her go away," I said to Elsa. "Forever."

Elsa nodded, but then she rocked on the couch, back and forth, her brows knit together. It wasn't a good sign. Kitty's breath hitched and we locked eyes. A string of songs warbled from Elsa's throat.

"I love your birds," I said. "They're really pretty." Elsa sprung up from the couch and went to her shelves, her fingertip tapping every figurine on the head in order from left to right. It would take her all morning to do all of them, and I hoped I hadn't ruined my chance for a conversation.

Then I remembered that I had Mary's necklace and the letter Lydia gave me in my Windbreaker pocket. The necklace could be a problem, if she recognized it as Mary's, but the letter never mentioned Mary by name. It seemed a safer bet.

"Elsa, I have a letter that you might want to look at? If not, that's okay."

Elsa stopped with the birds and turned to look at me. She glanced over at Karen. The blanket had fallen off of Karen's shoulders to puddle on the floor, and Elsa rushed over to fuss with it, tucking the ends under Karen's arms with no help from the woman herself.

The tea remained untouched, steaming by Karen's elbow.

I slid the letter across the wicker table. Elsa resumed her position across from us. She eyed the envelope awhile before opening the letter from Seymour Hawthorne to Elizabeth. I braced for the worst, but she calmly refolded it, reinserted it, and slid it back to me.

And put the bird on my head. It fell to the floor. She pointed at it and then me.

Kitty stooped to retrieve it, her look equal parts confusion and frustration. I felt the same, but I wasn't sure what to do. In the end, it didn't matter. Elsa let out a cry, standing from the couch so fast, I was afraid she'd hit her head on the overhead ceiling fan. She whirled in a circle, the floral muumuu billowing out around her before she sailed to the windows. She started at the left window, her hands pressed against the contact paper before she inched to the right and swept across the room, narrowly avoiding Karen.

"Elsa? Is everything okay?" I was alarmed. So was Kitty. She crept off the couch to retreat toward the intercom on the wall.

Elsa moaned, the fingers of her right hand spreading over the glass. She shoved her face against the pane, nose mashing flat. Behind me, Kitty pushed the button to call Nurse Lacy. The intercom buzzed as Elsa let out a low-pitched bellow. I eased her way, hoping to bring comfort—terrified that I'd tormented her with the letter—but before I could reach her, Elsa screeched and bashed her head against the glass.

Crunch.

She sobbed and pulled back for a second strike, the contact hard enough to shake the window without breaking it.

Crunch!

Blood splashed across the contact paper, following the bubbling pattern as it dribbled down.

Crunch, crunch, crunch.

"Elsa, no!" My arms wrapped around her from behind. I heaved her back, but she was heavier than me and so much stronger. Her head slammed off the glass again and again, her nose exploding in a burst of red. She wailed, both her natural hand and her prosthetic beating on the glass above her head. I slid my hand between her face and the window to stop her, but she crushed my fingers with her next blow.

I yelped and pulled away, my forearm covered in Elsa's blood. Behind me, Kitty pounded on the buzzer for assistance, opening the door and screaming for help. Nurse Lacy burst in a few seconds later, a young, redheaded nurse on his heels. The blood was everywhere—on Elsa, on me. It covered the pane and soiled the carpet below. Splashes of it traveled far enough that they dappled Karen's cheek.

"What happened?" Nurse Lacy demanded, he and the other nurse wrapping their arms around Elsa to peel her away from the window.

"I don't know. I'm sorry. She got up and . . . I don't know." Tears streamed down my cheeks. My fingers ached. Elsa thrashed to get away from them, but when Nurse Lacy whispered in her ear, she went slack and sobbed. The nurses turned her around and guided her to the couch.

"Sign out," Nurse Lacy said. "Please. At the front desk. I have to take care of her. You can leave the lanyards there."

"I . . . right. I swear, I didn't do anything."

He said nothing. I took two steps back before Elsa lifted her pulpy, smashed face my way, her nose crushed and pointing at an odd angle. She whimpered and then she screeched, furious, blood and spittle flying in my direction. I understood then why she could hum but not talk.

Elsa Samburg had no tongue.

21

"I don't know what happened." I dropped Elsa's trinkets into the basket outside of her room, the tears drying on my cheeks. "She seemed fine with the letter. I don't get it."

"Neither do I, but you have to call the sheriff," Kitty said. "Maybe if he hears it from you, he won't be so mad."

The idea felt as bad as when I'd had to call my mother to tell her Bronx had fallen through the windows from our apartment—or been pushed by Mary, really.

The blood drying on my arms felt itchy. I wanted to stop by a bathroom to scrub, but I was pretty sure if we didn't exit immediately, Nurse Lacy would call security. We removed our lanyards and signed out at the unattended desk, baffled by Elsa's breakdown.

The mystery was solved the moment we stepped outside.

Jess stood on the brick walkway, peering at the building front. Her head was bandaged above the ears, her lip and eye still swollen from the previous day's attack. The bruises on her face and neck had faded from plum to a sickly yellow. She wore a too-big Harvard sweatshirt and sweatpants, which had to be loaners from her aunt.

Seeing all the blood on me, her eyes went huge. "Oh, God. Did Mary attack you? I'm so sorry."

"What are you doing here?" I stalked toward her, anger surging from the pit of my stomach like lava bubbling up inside of a volcano. "You were told to stay away."

She took a step back. "I'm sorry. I just wanted to talk to her myself. Probably about the same stuff you were talking to her about, but I felt useless at home."

"You were told to stay away!" My hands made contact with her shoulders, and I shoved as hard as I could. She fell back into a pink flowering bush, flailing, her feet barely touching the ground. "Why don't you listen?"

Elsa had been fine. If she was prone to violence or self-harm they would have warned me or not let me come at all. Something outside the window had set her off. Elsa sensed the Mary taint. She knew evil was in her midst and she reacted to it.

"Shauna," Kitty said from behind me, her voice quiet. "We should go."

"I cannot believe you, Jess." I closed in on her and grabbed her shoulders, my fingers digging in so hard that she flinched. I shook her, my body convulsing with rage. "Your aunt told you why you shouldn't come. You hurt Elsa."

"I deserve to talk to her!" Jess yelled it in my face, pushing me back. "She's got answers. I'm the one dying here."

"Elsa just smashed her face to bits. The blood on me is hers. Do you know why? It's because YOU showed up after Dell told you it was a bad idea. I keep wanting to forgive you—to find something redeemable about you—and you keep acting as if your life is worth more than everyone else's!"

"I tried to save you before! From Mary. I did that for you," she protested. She reached out her hand to me, to touch my arm, but I recoiled.

"No, you did it for *you*. You didn't want to lose *your* friend. It'd inconvenience *you*. Anna and Kitty were incidental to *your* needs. I guess Cody was, too, huh?" I stepped into Jess again, seething enough my fist clenched, but Kitty grabbed the back of my shirt and yanked.

"Let's go." She walked me toward the parking lot, her hand looped around my bicep. It didn't hurt, but her grip was firm enough that I didn't dare struggle, either.

"I'm okay," I lied.

"No, you're not. People are staring. Get in the car." Kitty threw me into the passenger's side of the SUV before whirling on Jess, her finger lifting to point at her face. "We're going to see Dell to tell her what happened with Elsa, and after that you're going to stay away from us, or I swear to God I'll feed you to Mary myself."

Jess dropped her head into her hands and wept, soul-wrenching sobs that echoed across the grounds. I jerked my face away, angry and hurt and sad.

Why, Jess? I want to open up to you again, but you keep screwing it up.

Smatters of elderly people watched us, some through the windows, some on morning walks. Most of them looked concerned, but a few were clearly scared. One woman gesticulated at us with a cell phone attached to her ear.

My mouth screwed into an ugly smirk.

By all means, call the cops. I'm sure the sheriff is going to love hearing this.

∞

She hadn't called the sheriff, or if she had, he wasn't off the phone with her by the time I called. I got his voice mail instead. I rambled through my explanation, apologizing every other sentence and laying a whole heap of blame on Jess's shoulders.

"The nerve." I slid my phone into my pocket. I'd wanted to believe Jess was getting better, but a leopard doesn't change its spots. "I wonder if she tried to talk to Elsa after we left. I hope not, for Elsa's sake." Kitty shook her head, guiding the car onto Dell's street.

We parked the car at ten o'clock sharp according to the dashboard. I pulled out Seymour Hawthorne's letter and approached the front door.

I knocked, alarmed when the door swung open with barely any pressure. I pushed it all the way, and Horace rushed past me and dove under the porch. Something wasn't right. An unpleasant coldness settled into my chest.

Mary.

Kitty took a step forward, but I held her back, a finger lifting to my lips to indicate quiet. She nodded, wide-eyed.

Snort. Snuffle. Gurgle.

Wet, animalistic sounds resonated from the back of the house, Dell's kitchen. I surveyed the living room. Everything was orderly as it should be, no pictures out of place, no tchotchkes skewed. The mess we'd made with the Mary memorabilia had been tidied, the accordion folders lined up neatly. Only a single letter remained out in the open. The box of salt and the candle from yesterday's failed summoning were perched on the end of the stairs, waiting to be put away.

Another snort from the kitchen was followed by a ragged moan. Even wordless, I recognized Dell's voice.

She's alive back there.

But she wasn't alone, and by the sounds of it, Mary had done something awful to her.

Kitty and I had a choice to make. We shared a look before she squeezed my fingers. I squeezed back. She went for the box of salt on the stairs as I tiptoed toward the fireplace, grabbing the poker from the kit by the mantel. I lifted it as carefully as I could, not wanting to rattle or clang and call attention our way. The iron weight in my hands was a small comfort as I eased toward the hallway, my feet silent on the rug. Kitty followed so close behind me, I could feel the heat of her breath on the back of my ear.

Out of the living room and past the bathroom. The mauve carpet ended at the doorway of the kitchen, becoming beige linoleum. The smears were impossible to miss. Wide, thick rust smudges streaked the floor, as if someone had taken a push

broom to a puddle of blood. It traversed the kitchen from right
to left and curled up and around the island toward the sliding
back doors. The left door was broken, the glass shattered at the
top with angry, pointed shards lining the bottom.

I eased inside and immediately wished I hadn't. Mary
crouched above Dell's supine body, squatting like a troll over
fleshy treasure. Her feet flanked Dell's torso, pinning her arms
tight. Mary's head was tilted forward hiding her expression, the
gaping hole of her ear allowing a beetle to scurry in and out
with wild abandon. Her dress was no longer white, but brown
from crusted sand.

She climbed out of the pit. She found a way.

I bit my tongue to keep from crying out.

There was another wet squish, and Dell screamed—a
strange, muffled thing that sounded off. I couldn't see what
Mary had done, but Dell's legs and hands juddered, slapping
against the floor beneath her. A puddle of blood-tinged water
dribbled across the floor, settling into the grooves between the
tiles and slithering toward my sneaker.

I cringed and eyed Kitty. She swallowed hard and nodded, encouraging me forward. I raised the fireplace poker over
my head.

Another inch to the left.

Two.

The moment I had a clear view of what Mary had done to
Dell, I had to bite back my screams. One of Mary's hands pried
Dell's mouth open too wide. Her thumb peeled up Dell's top lip,

exposing a row of gums missing half their teeth. I was frozen in terror, unable to look away as Mary reached in to pluck another tooth free with her bare fingers.

Squish.

Dell howled, body bowing in agony. Mary ignored her pain, stuffing the tooth into her own fetid maw with a series of chuffs.

She's taking Dell's teeth.

"No," I wheezed, my brain refusing to accept the scene before me. "No!"

Mary jerked her face my way and hissed, her lower face smeared with Dell's blood, the top line of her teeth red-stained porcelain.

22

I charged Mary, the fireplace poker clenched in my fists like a baseball bat. I arced it down, swinging at her head as hard as I could, but Mary jerked out her hand to intercept the blow. She tore the iron from my grasp with ease and tossed it aside like garbage. It clanged as it hit the refrigerator, rolling under the kitchen cabinets and from my reach.

Kitty rushed in with the salt. Handful after handful, smoke billowing from Mary's head where it struck cursed flesh. Mary screeched, her claws tearing tracks in her own face. The flayed flesh gaped wide, a black, tarry blood seeping from the wounds. The kitchen reeked, a cross between spoiled milk and burnt meat.

"Get the poker!" Kitty barked, advancing. Mary stumbled when Dell reached up to grab her foot and twist. It wasn't enough to trip her, but it was enough to call her attention to the floor. She snarled and reached down, face still smoking when she bunched her hands in the front of Dell's bloodied pajama top.

I darted for the poker as Kitty ripped open the top of the salt box, shaking the contents over the top of Mary's bald, pointed head. Another barrage of smoke accompanied her scream. Dell dropped to the floor with a wet thud.

Mary retreated toward the doors. The smoke pouring off of her spread across the ceiling. I grabbed the poker, holding it like a rapier as my sneaker skidded through the growing puddle on the floor. Water was everywhere. I couldn't tell if it was from Mary's time in the swamp or part of her ghostly repertoire.

I lunged at her. She swiped at me again before grabbing a kitchen chair, hoisting it like it weighed nothing. The chair sailed at my head, but I ducked, feeling the brush of air as it whizzed by my ear. The chair hit the wall and splintered apart, leaving a huge dent in the plaster.

I skittered forward with the poker in one hand. Kitty flanked from the other side, now armed with the table salt. Mary swung her head between us, gurgling before her mouth curled up into her new smile. She grabbed a chair in each hand and whipped them—one at me, the other at Kitty. I heard Kitty scream as I dove for the floor, the chair striking the cabinets above me and raining down wooden pieces.

Chair legs, armrests, and the seat pelted me on the back. Mary ran at me, her engorged foot slamming down on the wrist of the hand holding the weapon. Her claws plunged into my back. She sunk them deep, through my Windbreaker, thin T-shirt, and bra, cutting through flesh and muscle.

I screamed as she tittered above me. Mary wrested one of her hands from my back to twist it around the base of my ponytail, lifting me by it, all of my weight pulling on my scalp. She hauled me close, pressing my fleshy body against her bony one. Her head dipped close to mine as she breathed in my scent.

Or, more specifically, the scent of my blood. She twitched beside me and then she lifted her head, striking down like a viper, her new teeth sinking into the meat of my shoulder.

She bit me. The bitch bit me!

I keened. I didn't know if I was marked again, if the burden had bounced back my way. Mary reared up, a splash of my blood joining the rest on her mouth. I thrashed in her arms, but Mary squeezed tighter, her hand leaving my ponytail to stroke over the top of my head. Her fingers threaded through the strands as if to comb them. She wrapped a lock around her bony, blue finger and pulled, watching it bounce up. She repeated the gesture, chortling as my hair resumed its shape upon release. The third time, she wound it tight before jerking it from my head.

The lock ripped away. Hot blood rushed down my scalp. It coiled over my forehead and dripped along my cheek. My vision swam, refocusing in time to see Mary lifting a lock of my hair to her own head, like she'd fashioned herself a new wig.

My understanding was swift and brutal.

She wants my hair.

"NO. IT'S MINE. YOU CAN'T HAVE IT!"

Mary shook me to silence me, cooing as she gazed at the red curls surrounding my face. I kicked her knee. I pinched her sides. I fought her with every bit of strength I could claim. It did nothing.

What did do something was the knife.

Neither Mary nor I saw Kitty coming. One second she wasn't there, the next she was, jamming the butcher's knife at Mary with a scream. Mary dropped me, my legs unable to right themselves in time to keep me upright. I hit the floor with a whump, sprawling beside Dell and feeling queasy.

The poker. Have to get the poker.

I gritted my teeth and crawled across the kitchen floor. Kitty pulled the knife free, only to plunge it in again—higher and farther than the first strike. Stabs like that would have killed a person, but Mary was different. Nonhuman. She flailed, her arms swinging wildly to either side of her, knocking candlesticks and a napkin holder off the kitchen table.

My hand closed around the iron.

I swung it around as hard as I could, smashing Mary in the leg. She staggered back, twisting her body to avoid another blow. Instead of facing the kitchen, she faced the shattered sliding doors. I hit her again, aiming for the second knee. She fell forward. I didn't intend for her to hit the jagged spikes of the glass door, but that's how she landed, the longest, thickest pieces impaling her chest and stomach. Her lower half kicked behind her, her upper half pounded on the planks of the deck.

"Oh, my God. Are you okay?" Kitty sailed to my side, a nasty cut bleeding on the side of her neck.

"Yes. No. I don't know. Dell." I motioned toward Dell. She'd rolled onto her hip, away from me. Her back was unmarred, but I knew the devastation of the front. I crawled over to her, putting my hand on her shoulder. "I am so sorry."

It was unclear how long Mary would be out of commission. Part of me wanted to stab her a few hundred more times, but her powers of recuperation were so ridiculous, the better plan was to run while we had the chance.

Dell shouted something back at me, but without her top teeth, I couldn't understand her. She slapped at the floor in front of her. I scrambled around to her front side, still kneeling. She gazed at me with watery eyes, her mouth closed but seeping blood from the corners. She tried to speak again, but it came out like a moan. Frustrated, she growled before forcing herself up onto an elbow.

She dipped her finger in the blood beneath her and wrote on the linoleum.

L.

E.

T.

"Letter," I said, remembering the letter on the table in the front room. Dell nodded and cringed. I shoved myself up and glanced back at Mary. She thrashed like an upended roach, occasionally pushing herself far enough up the spikes that she'd free herself from one only to slip down to the bottom of another.

"We have to go now," I said to Kitty. "Help Dell."

We maneuvered to either side of Dell, adopting the all-too-familiar position of carrying one of our wounded when she couldn't propel herself. Out of the kitchen and into the hallway, the space was too narrow for three adult bodies and so we turned to the side, sidled our way to the living room. Once there, I broke away to grab the letter, stuffing it into the pocket with Mary's locket.

We hurried out of the house and to the SUV.

"What about the cat?" Kitty asked, helping Dell into the backseat. "Should I try to coax him out from under the porch?"

"Screw the cat. We have to go." Kitty glared at me before climbing into the driver's side, waiting for me to take my seat before locking the doors. She peeled away from Dell's house with a cloud of dust and screeching tires. "Fine. Where are we going?"

"To the hospital," I said.

Dell grunted from the backseat, slapping the headrest next to my ear. I turned to look at her. She put up two fingers, then one finger before pantomiming making a call and pointing back at her house.

"Jess," I said, my voice flat. "You want me to warn her."

Dell nodded and collapsed into the backseat. The blood at the sides of her mouth made me think of a clown with a painted frown.

I pulled out my phone, the message difficult to type because my hands shook so badly, I could barely function.

Stay away from Dell's. Mary is there. Dell w/us.

The moment I sent it, Dell tapped my headrest again. This time, she pointed at my pocket.

"Yes, the letter, but you need to get to the hosp—" She shook her head and poked my pocket, jabbing me in the hip.

Joseph,

My sweet man. Please come home. Of course I will think no worse of you for it. I know what I charged you with in my previous letters, but that was revenge speaking. If it added undue pressure, I'm sorry. I'm grateful for all you have done. Solomon's Folly is an unpleasant place in the best of circumstances. In the worst, it's nightmarish. You've spent two long months righting the wrongs done to my sister and mother. It's not your fault that you were stymied at every pass.

While I've never met the pastor myself, my sister's letters were enough to convince me that he is a demon. I'm glad you find him displeasing. It would have troubled me more, I think, if you'd disagreed with Mary's assessment. To know that he's as dogmatic and unpleasant as Mary claimed is a strange comfort. I can cast him as a villain with no weight upon my conscience.

I cannot say much about the Hawthornes other than what you've gleaned. Seymour is protective of his house and something of an ass (forgive me, I know that's awful). It's sad that a servant of justice would be so corrupt. You're likely right about the family's involvement. Elizabeth was always cruel to Mary, and her marriage to the pastor makes me believe more than ever they have something to hide. It's not so surprising, I suppose. The Hawthornes' legacy is mysterious and dismal.

The constable isn't a terrible man if you don't expect him to do his duty. Mother often had him to dinner. The best I can say about him is he's a jovial drunk and a terrible card cheat. You do know he spends his weekends at the gentlemen's club with Seymour? That would explain why your attempts to get into Hawthorne House went unsupported. He is in Seymour's pocket, as snug as a ball of lint.

I am glad you will pursue the matter beyond Seymour's authority. I don't expect the state to do much about it, but at least we tried. I don't want to give up without a fight. I already feel like we were bullied away from the truth.

Your return is joyful for you, for me, and for our son. You will be happy to know he is past his croup. He is hardy and hale and quite eager to see his father after so long. This awfulness denied you much-deserved time, and I am eager to see you reacquainted.

I will see you soon, my love.

Constance

23

I read the letter once, and then I read it aloud for Kitty. Seymour Hawthorne's letter came next for Dell. I reopened the letter Jess forwarded to me on the phone from Philip Starkcrowe to Constance, too. I wished I had the rest, but I wasn't sure I needed them anymore. The puzzle pieces that had been straining to fit for so long clicked together in one glorious, terrible moment of understanding.

Philip's letter to Constance after her disappearance. Joseph's letter to Constance telling her of the search. Seymour Hawthorne's letter to Elizabeth Hawthorne telling her she'd marry Starkcrowe. Constance to Joseph telling him to come home. Constance to Joseph six months later, after he'd left The Folly, telling him she'd seen Mary's ghost.

"I know where she is," I said, my voice strangled. "Oh, my God. Elsa tried to tell me, and I was too stupid to figure it out."

"What are you talking about? What does Elsa have to do with anything?" Kitty looked alarmed, as if I spoke in tongues.

"It's Hawthorne House!" I scrambled with the letters. "Okay, this last letter, Constance says Joseph was never given permission to look in Hawthorne House. One of the earlier letters—I think it's in Dell's collection—says that he got a warrant for the church. But he must have been stopped when he tried to get another one to investigate the Hawthornes. And in Seymour's letter, he talks about the House of Hawthorne all with capital *H*s. But then he says in one line, 'I dislike having this stain under my crest. It befouls my house,' with a little *h*. He means the actual house, not the family. The crest is the bird. The stain is Mary. They must have moved Mary from the church to the house."

Kitty grinned beside me, slapping the steering wheel and bouncing in her seat. "The bird in the window is the crest! Elsa kept putting you under the bird. Holy shit. Okay, okay. So now what?"

"We'll get Dell to the hospital and then I'll call—"

Another smack to my headrest. Dell shook her head at me from the backseat, stubbornly refusing to be sent away. She didn't look good; her coloring was gray, her brow sweaty. I reached out to check her for fever, and she was clammy to the touch. Every part of her drooped, as if she'd gone boneless since the attack.

"You need a doctor," Kitty said looking at Dell in the rearview. "You look awful."

Dell's hand lifted and she made her fingers walk, then mimed the phone call again. It took me a second to decipher it. "You want us to go there and then call? The sher—no, an ambulance. Right. Okay." She tapped her nose and slumped into her seat.

"Two birds, one stone," I said. "Head to Hawthorne House. Or, no. Wait. Mary. She bled me. I don't know if she's going to follow me or not, and Lydia and Bran are there. Maybe you two should go without me."

"No way." Kitty stopped driving in the vague direction of *away from Dell's* and toward the highway that'd get us to Hawthorne House. "Dell's just as apt to have Mary on her trail as you are at this point, and I don't want to go alone. Sorry, don't mean to endanger the Hawthornes, but this is not a one-man job."

That meant I needed to convince Sheriff Hawthorne to let us dig around his house *and* relocate his children.

"What if he doesn't let us in?" I squirmed in my seat, immediately regretting it when my back ached. I went stone still to lessen the pain. "He doesn't have to cooperate."

Dell slapped her palm over her chest, her brow furrowed. She looked fierce. I remembered then what she'd said when she'd first put in the call to Hawthorne.

His blood owes mine and I'm not afraid to remind him.

I called, hoping the sheriff wouldn't avoid me after the morning's episode with Elsa. He picked up after one ring.

"Hawthorne." He sounded harsh.

"Hi, Sheriff. It's Shauna. I called earlier."

"I know. The facility called, too. Karen's fine. I should have known better, but—" He cut himself off. "It's not your fault. They left you unsupervised and that wasn't—it's not your fault."

"Thanks." I sucked in a deep breath as Kitty pulled onto the highway. At most, we were ten minutes away from the manor house. I couldn't waste any time. "Look, there's no good way to tell you this, so I'm just going to get to it. I think Mary's body is in Hawthorne House. Like, buried in it somewhere."

There was a long pause on the other end of the line. "What makes you say that?"

I couldn't read his voice. He didn't sound mad, but that didn't mean he wasn't. "Letters we've read. We dug up Mary's locket in the church. We think she might have been buried there at one point. I'd love to show you everything, but there's no time now. Mary killed Anna and Cody. She beat up Dell. God, she pulled out her teeth. It's now or never, Sheriff. Please."

He said nothing for a long moment, but then I heard the whir of police car sirens. "Give me twenty minutes to collect my kids. I'll unlock the chains. If you're looking for clues, they'd be in the old house."

We waited in a convenience store parking lot off the highway. It was a run-down place with one functioning gas pump that had no credit card slider, a neon OPEN sign blinking in the window, and another sign warning shoplifters they'd be persecuted above a picture of a shotgun. A Rottweiler trotted around the back of the store on a short leash, barking at us.

The sheriff needed time to get his kids out. It occurred to me that he could be sweeping the house to try to hide evidence. Was twenty minutes long enough to move a body? What choice did I have but to believe him when he said he wanted one less monster in town? Dell shivered in the backseat. Kitty cranked the heat despite the June temperature pushing eighty. It wouldn't do a whole lot against shock.

"The minute we get there, I'm calling nine-one-one," Kitty said. A part of me could understand why Dell made a fuss. She'd been victimized by Mary off and on for fifty years—she didn't want to be sent away at the last minute.

Five more minutes. I was about to tell Kitty to head toward the house when my phone buzzed. Jess.

"Where are you?" she asked.

"On our way to Hawthorne House. We'll call an ambulance for Dell when we get there."

"Why are you waiting?" Jess sounded furious, like we were denying care to Dell just to spite her. As usual, it was all about Jess.

"I can't put her on the phone. She can't talk. Mary pulled out her teeth. She insisted she come along." I glanced at the backseat. Dell's head dipped forward, her eyes fluttering. "Or, we'll call now and the ambulance can meet us there. Either way, she'll get to the hospital."

"Fine." Jess hung up. I wondered if I should warn her away from Hawthorne House, but what good would it do? She didn't listen to anybody. My lone consolation was that she posed no greater or lesser threat than I did. Mary had bled me and I'd survived. I could be her chosen victim.

Again.

"She's going to meet us there, I take it," Kitty said, her voice flat.

"Probably."

Kitty started the car and drove us out of the parking lot. I dialed 911 on my phone, but before the call went through, Dell's hand swatted out to smack the phone away. It fell into the well beside my feet. She scowled at me and shook her head.

"You're being stubborn," I said. She shrugged. "If you die, Mary wins."

We'd just pulled onto the winding road that led to the sheriff's house when Kitty squinted at her rearview. Her eyes swept from street to mirror and back again, her spine stiffening. I looked behind me. I could see the dot on the horizon, far enough away that it was indiscernible, close enough that it lent me pause.

"Is it—?"

"I don't know," I said, cutting Kitty off. "But we'd best be prepared." I did a cursory check of the backseat for makeshift weapons. Salt. So much salt. We had the shovel and sledgehammer from the basement excavation along with the lanterns and lighters. I picked up a lantern and turned it over. Lamp oil.

I didn't know if Bloody Mary could burn, but I wasn't beyond finding out.

24

Hawthorne House vacant was dreadful.

The tall grass in the fields should have rustled. Birds should have sung from their perches in the trees. The wind should have whispered as it blew by, but everything was still. I climbed from the car, a lantern in my hand, a lighter wedged into the waistband of my jeans, my pockets bulging with salt.

I expected Dell to wait in the car, but as soon as Kitty parked, Dell started limping toward the older half of Hawthorne House. She was in better shape than I assumed, or maybe this was like her perseverance in the swamp—Aunt Dell was Herculean. There was flint under that withered exterior.

"I'm still calling an ambulance," Kitty said. "She's hurt."

"I'll go with her." I jogged across the yard. Dell was already at the house, stepping over the rusty coils of chains that had barred the way not an hour ago. She turned the knob and the door swung wide on the hinge. The interior of the house was so dark, I was sure it was where light went to die. I shouted at Dell to stop, shoving past her to take the lead.

"You're hurt and I have a light. Let me go first."

She nodded, the movement sending flakes of dried blood snowing to the ground. The crease between her lips remained a brilliant scarlet.

I searched for light switches along the wall, but flicking them did nothing. I lit the lantern, thankful for its dim incandescence. It was strange to be in a house so similar to the other while being altogether different at the same time. The layouts matched, the front room and kitchen that opened up on the right to a dining room. The stairs were on the left, a bathroom tucked in behind. The open archway in front of the staircase led into a den.

But the floorboards curled up in the corners. Dingy sheets shrouded the furniture. The chandelier above the entrance had nine broken flutes of glass surrounding nine equally-as-broken lightbulbs. I was afraid a rotten floor might send me plummeting into the basement, but a few slow, steady steps proved the construction solid. I swept the kitchen, Dell shivering all the while. Her hand balled in my shirt. She tugged too hard, forcing the fabric to brush over my new cuts.

I opened cabinets and poked my head into the bathroom. Raw pipes from where a vanity used to be. A lime-stained toilet. A moth-eaten shower curtain hid a tub with curved white feet. I whisked it aside, but the tub was empty save for disassembled plumbing guts.

Too obvious. If they hid the body, they actually hid it. Crawl spaces. Under floorboards. In closets.

I edged my way to the steps, Dell my frail shadow.

"I'm going for the basement," I said to her. "Be careful."

Dell grabbed my arm and shook her head, pointing at a broken board in the floor near the kitchen. I shone my flashlight down, only to see a dirt floor. Dell poked me again and proceeded to hold her fingers close together, pantomiming small.

"A small basement?"

She nodded. Her hands closed together one on top, one on the bottom like a sandwich.

"A crawl space?"

She nodded once.

I didn't have the resources to handle a crawl space, and our time frame wasn't exactly solid. I swept the downstairs instead. Going into the side room, I found a small door tucked in the corner that looked like it had been purposefully hidden by a chair. I moved the chair and looked inside, the dim light making it hard to see.

There was a scratching sound and I tensed, my hand poised on the short half door. A mouse scurried into my flashlight light, eyes big and whiskers twitching.

My heart is racing over a rodent. Breathe, Shauna. Get it together.

I headed back for the entryway so I could climb to the second floor. Dell had taken the other side of the house, but when I moved for the stairs, she followed.

"Nothing?" I asked.

She shook her head.

The stair rail felt solid beneath my hand. I climbed to the second story, Dell at my back. A jingle outside made me tense, but then Kitty jogged in behind us with the sledgehammer clenched in her hands. She eyeballed the stairs before whirling on the window to her left, knocking two boards away from the glassless frame. Shards of light stretched across the dark, gouged floor.

Kitty followed us up the stairs. "That's better. The operator said fifteen or twenty minutes on the ambulance. Maybe you should wait in the car, Dell?"

Dell didn't answer.

Up we went. The spiderwebs on the second story were intense, stretched from the ceiling beams to the railing on the balcony over the kitchen. I used the lantern to sweep them aside. Sticky white strands clung to my arm and tangled in my hair. A wisp flew into my mouth. "It's possible Elsa was being literal. Maybe Mary's under the stained glass window," I said. "Or maybe she's under one of the tombstones in the graveyard."

Dell tugged on my sleeve and pointed past me. At the back of the room, a slim door nestled in beside a sheet-covered bookshelf. I hefted the lantern and approached. The door opened with no trouble, though the stairs beyond were daunting. The boards were narrow and steep, twisting up into blackness.

My shoulders barely fit as I ascended. The darkness abated the higher we climbed, light peeking in through tiny cracks in the walls. Two rotations up and I had to stop. An overhead door blocked the way. I jiggled the hook latch, but it wouldn't move.

"Kitty, I need the sledgehammer." She handed it to me without complaint.

I gripped it by the handle and shoved up, once, twice. Metal moaned in protest before the door flew open with a loud rattle, kicking up a cloud of dust. I pulled my T-shirt up over my nose so I wouldn't have to breathe it in and climbed into the room.

The space was twelve feet wide but only eight deep. Windows faced the front yard and to the east. To the west, a glass door gave access to the widow's walk. The stained glass window should have been on the south side, but it was shielded by a wall. Two broken end tables, a covered couch, and a faded painting of flowers barred the way.

The stained glass wasn't dark from dust. It's dark because it's walled off from the other windows.

"Maybe she's behind it," I said. "They could have hid her there."

Outside, a screech echoed across the Hawthorne property.

⌒⌒

Knowing who it was—how close she was—I rushed to action. When the door to the widow's walk wouldn't open, I used the sledgehammer to force it, breaking three panes of glass in the process. The sheriff's potential ire didn't matter. Nothing mattered except getting behind that wall.

"Move the furniture," I said. "We need to get at the window."

"Just toss it out on the widow's walk?" Kitty tested the couch with her foot before stepping on it and grabbing the painting from the wall.

"Yes. Hurry."

Dell stood back while Kitty and I cleared the room. The couch wouldn't fit through the doorframe, so we maneuvered it over the floor hatch as a Mary deterrent. I was afraid the wall blocking us from the window was constructed of brick, like something from "The Cask of Amontillado," but there was a fist-sized hole near the bottom. Something had scratched its way through the horsehair plaster, allowing a shred of light to pass into our side of the cupola.

I swung the sledgehammer around with all my strength. The wall gave way more easily than I'd expected, the old plaster crumbling upon impact. The second strike sent white bits flying around the room like shrapnel. Over and over I pounded, until we could see the skeletal wooden framework beneath.

Until we could see a brown leather trunk behind the wall.

It was about five feet long, two wide, two deep. Black straps at the ends held it closed, the golden buckles gleaming despite ages of disuse. In front of it was an aged, yellow envelope face-down on the floor.

"Oh, God." I cleared out enough of the bottom plaster that I could step into the hidden portion of the cupola. I tucked the envelope in my back pocket and crouched beside the trunk, the sledgehammer propped against the wall behind me. My eyes strayed to the glass window above with its black bird. The crow's beady eyes watched me.

Another bellow from outside impelled me to open the trunk. I went for the lock expecting it to give me trouble, but the moment I applied pressure, it opened. The lid parted from the base and a musty odor filled the air.

Kitty lifted the lantern, the light revealing a 150-year-old truth. Bones and cloth. Ragged yellow lace twisted around a pile of remains so long interred, there was no flesh. To the left, a skull with crooked teeth. A leg bone. A pile of dust. To the right, a rib cage, a scrap of black cloth . . .

And a second skull. There wasn't supposed to be a second skull.

My hand flew to my mouth.

"Oh, Jesus."

"Is that two skulls?" Kitty demanded. "Oh, my God. Who is it?"

My mind raced for an explanation. Names and dates streamed through my head. Constance and Joseph lived to ripe old ages. We'd found Hannah in the cave. Elizabeth was buried outside. The friends were accounted for even if we hadn't seen their grave markers in person.

Starkcrowe went missing. His tombstone said he died April 8, 1865.

Something about the date seemed significant, and I racked my brain, trying to force the connection.

"April eighth. April eighth." I murmured it to myself, my mind's eye retracing all the steps I'd made in my Mary journey.

"What?" Kitty demanded.

Constance.

"The letter!" I nearly squawked it, turning back to the remains. "From Constance to Joseph."

Mary moaned somewhere below us, the encroaching threat working her way toward the humans trapped in the small space. Kitty tossed one of the end tables onto the couch, like that'd help keep Mary out.

"Which letter? Spit it out, Shauna."

"It was dated April ninth. Constance saw Mary for the first time the day after Starkcrowe's supposed disappearance. Don't you get it?"

Frantic, I thrust my hands into the bones, searching for answers. The yellow lace was definitely from a woman's dress, but the black cloth was nondescript. I moved aside the rib cage and grabbed for what looked like a sleeve. The bones rattled as I pulled it free. The cloth was thin and yet still managed to be stiff. I oriented it as best I could, wincing when a bone dropped from inside to join the collection below.

It was a jacket adorned with brass buttons, the folded lapels reminding me of a gentleman's suit coat. Layered beneath was a clerical collar.

"It's Starkcrowe," I said. "Mary's spirit rose six months after her death. When they buried her with her murderer."

Mary chose to stay.

The Hawthornes' cruelty birthed this monster.

25

From downstairs came the crash of a marauding ghost breaking furniture. I dropped the pastor's coat and eyed the remains, my pulse pounding in my ears. There was no way out of here. The widow's walk was on the roof of the house, and while the eaves allowed us to slide down a ways, it was a long drop to the ground.

Except for the conservatory. It was tall enough. If we can get a solid grip, it'd be possible to jump.

"Take Dell to the conservatory and climb down. I'll burn the bodies. Maybe destroying the remains will send her away." I removed the cap from the bottom of the lantern, a slow trickle of lamp oil escaping the hole. I sloshed it over the bones and ancient clothes. "I really hope they send a fire truck along with the ambulance. Otherwise, the whole house will burn."

More thunderous noises from downstairs and the sound of

something heavy breaking. Mary hunted us, and the longer she went without her quarry, the angrier she grew.

"The conservatory's in ruins, Shauna. The dome's broken. The broken glass. How are we supposed to—"

"It's better to risk that than stay here," I yelled. "Just head that way, Kitty. I'll catch up to you, okay?" On the outside, I was stone. On the inside, I was mush. But we'd come too far to fail. We were closer to ending Mary's curse than anyone had ever come before.

I resigned myself to the dangers a long time ago. I can do this.

Kitty grabbed Dell by the arm and pulled, but Dell's feet remained planted to the floor. Dell pointed at me and extended her hand for the lantern.

I eyed her. "I'll do it."

She opened her mouth to speak and another torrent of blood spilled forth. A clot slithered from between her lips and spilled onto her shirt. Her jaw snapped shut. She looked pained as she pointed out at the widow's walk and then smacked her bad leg.

"She can't do the climb," Kitty said quietly. "And I can't carry her alone."

Dell tapped the side of her nose. Again, she reached for the lantern. More stomping from below, this time on the stairs. The sofa atop the hatch would keep Mary out for a minute or two, but her strength was too great for it to last.

Our only hope is the bones.

I grabbed Dell's wrist and squeezed. "I'm going to lure her out so you can escape. I promise. Hang on as long as you can." Dell nodded. Kitty offered her the sledgehammer, but she declined, snatching the lantern and lighter from me. I tried to ignore the trembling of her hands and the ashen undertone to her skin.

Kitty charged out to the widow's walk. The railing had no break in it, so she made one with the sledgehammer, the piece skittering down to crash to the ground below. We paused on the edge of the roof and eyed the conservatory. Before, I'd been afraid to touch the rusty, twisted metal, but with Mary behind us and the promise of flames, I would risk it.

I eased along the ledge and toward the dome. A *fwump* and the smell of acrid smoke pulled my attention back to the cupola. Fire and the trumpeting squawk of an enraged ghost. We'd run out of time.

I slid down the roof's edge on my butt, pain ricocheting through my injured back with every bump. Kitty followed, the two of us careening far faster than intended. I kept hoping Mary would quiet behind us, whisked away from this plane and onto the next, but she screeched while the bones burned.

Near the end of the roof slope, I put out my hands to either side to slow me down. My palms burned where they scraped over the shingles. My sneaker caught on the second-story gutter just in time to stop me from sailing over. As Kitty skidded to a halt beside me, the gutter squealed and ripped away from the side of the house, sending us both scrambling back.

"Damn it." I glanced over at the conservatory four feet away.

"I'm going to go for it," I said. "I'll find something for you to jump down onto. A table or something."

Kitty looked between me and the metal dome. "Do you want me to try first?"

"No. I'm a little smaller and you've got the sledgehammer. Just... I'll be okay." I pushed myself up into a crouch, knowing I had to jump for all our sakes, but I couldn't make myself go. A countdown from three in my head did nothing to inspire the leap.

Dell's startled shout did. I looked back. Smoke poured from the open door of the cupola. The old woman staggered outside to the widow's walk, a hand held up in front of her. Mary emerged from the gray cloud like a chittering nightmare. The fact that her last tie to this world was licked by flames didn't appear to matter.

What if we were wrong? What if burning her body doesn't stop her?

I launched myself toward the conservatory. My legs kicked in the air, gravity threatening to splatter me across the hard, concrete floor a story below. A scream burst from my lips before my hands latched onto the curved metal of the dome. Something bit into my fingertips, the underside of the frame rusty and sharp, but I managed to cling, swinging back and forth like a pendulum.

I heaved my way toward another bar, body aching. Kitty shouted above. Mary snarled. Smoke wafted from the cupola door, thick and oily and hard to see through. I worked myself toward the ground as efficiently as possible, hopping to another bar. It bent beneath my weight but didn't tear away from the foundation. I moved closer to the crumbling podium of the old statue at the center of the conservatory. I dropped onto its flat surface.

I climbed outside the conservatory through a glassless panel in the window. Kitty shouted my name. I heard a shriek followed by a growl and a thud. Mary had closed in on them. Maybe she already had Dell. I had to entice her down.

"BLOODY MARY!" I screamed at the top of my lungs, running around the side of the house in hopes of luring her out through the front door. "BLOODY MARY, BLOODY MARY."

Mary bayed, a sound of outrage and despair that shredded the stillness of the farm. There was a yelp from the rooftop— Dell, I was pretty sure—and then Kitty screamed down to me.

"Run, Shauna! She's coming. Run!"

I turned the corner of the house as Mary hurtled off the roof, crashing into the ground six feet away from me.

The pile of dead girl twitched. All her parts looked out of place and haphazard. Her leg bent at an odd angle. One shoulder was higher than the other. A thumb pointed in the wrong direction on the hand. But it didn't stop her. Her tongue flicked out, like a snake tasting the air. She hoisted herself up onto her hands, then climbed to her feet, wet gurgles rattling from her chest.

I ran away from Hawthorne House, toward the fields. Mary snarled as she gave chase, lumbering after me despite her bony foot turned backward on the ankle. It flopped with her every step, the joints destroyed in the fall.

She was crippled, yes, but a healthy Mary was twice as fast as me. A broken Mary kept time, so close I could hear her wheezing breaths. I sprinted toward the closest field. It was the sole good field with its tidy fence, freshly tilled earth, and emerald grass.

The horizontal rails were spaced out enough that I could squeeze through and into the field with no problem. Mary lunged for me but didn't give chase. She'd cleared a roof to get me, she'd walked through fire to hurt my friends, but she wouldn't cross that fence. She hissed and screeched and slapped at the fence, but she wouldn't come after me.

I stopped and gasped for breath midfield, staring at Mary as she moved around the perimeter, snarling and testing the dirt. I looked down. Rich, dark earth. Nothing unusual about it.

Until it moved.

It was a subtle rumble at first—so slight it felt like vibrations on my heels. But then something wrenched beneath me, like the field turned itself. Fields weren't supposed to ripple. They weren't supposed to quicken when someone walked upon them. I took off running again, fear scratching at my skin from the inside.

What was it Jess had said about the swamp gas? Hard to imagine, but even Mary has her limits. Whatever lives in the Hawthornes' field is one of those limits.

I found the Hawthorne monster.

26

I ran, my breath short, my body slicked with sweat. Mary curved around from my right in an effort to cut me off. She lashed at me as I vaulted the fence, the edge of her pointed fingernail skimming the underside of my forearm. I raced down the driveway and past the second field. Sooner or later, I'd run out of steam and Mary wouldn't. I reached into my pockets for the salt, grabbing two fistfuls and tossing them back over my shoulders.

Mary screamed, pausing in her chase to contend with the burning flesh. It let me put a few yards between us, but it wasn't enough. I cleared another fence, the hip-tall grass slowing my progress. Mary jimmied a slat of broken fence from the post and threw it at me like a javelin. It went wide by a few feet. The second one came much, much closer, spiking into the ground beside my sneaker.

I fumbled in my pocket for the locket. Mary's locket. I whirled around and threw it sidearm at the ghost.

"IT'S YOURS, MARY. YOUR NECKLACE."

Mary snatched the necklace from the air and stopped cold, peering at the delicate thing gleaming against her palm. Her head tilted to the side and she cooed. It was the gentlest sound I'd ever heard from her. It was also the most unsettling.

I slowed my retreat, afraid any sudden movements would draw her attention from her new prize. I watched as Mary turned the necklace over to inspect the back. The remnants of her lips receded in what looked like a grimace, but the flutter of her one eyelid suggested something else.

Mary *was smiling*. That rotten countenance with its borrowed teeth *smiled*.

I continued backing away, my movements as unprovocative as I could make them. Mary ran her thumb along the crease of the locket. One of her serrated fingernails slid inside of it, springing the ancient mechanism and forcing it open.

All good vanished the moment she saw her pictures were gone. The portraits had been destroyed by time and the water under the church's floor. Mary threw the locket aside and tore after me with a fresh scream, her pace quickened by fury.

She blames me for the pictures. She thinks it's my fault.

Again I ran, this time through hip-height grass that pushed back at me. Mary lumbered after me like a rabid beast. She'd catch me soon, and I tried to steel myself for the fight I couldn't win. I was about to dive into the grass, hoping to hide beneath the underbrush, when the green Ford Focus turned onto the driveway.

Jess pressed her foot down on the gas and sped directly at us. Grit flew and tires squealed as she surged ahead. Jess crashed into Mary, sending her flying back twenty feet. She landed facedown, legs akimbo, but Jess didn't slow. She drove at Mary's prone body and then over it, squishing Mary into the dirt.

For the first time in a long time, I was glad to see Jess.

I scampered from the field and ran for the old house, cutting a wide berth around the ghoul. She writhed on the ground but hadn't recovered enough to pick herself back up again. Jess climbed from her car, a box of salt clenched in each hand. She rushed in to wave them over Mary's head and back, the smoke from the body a shadow of what billowed from the roof.

"What the hell happened?" she demanded as I ran up beside her.

I spoke through ragged breaths. "Dell burned the bones, but something's not working. She's still here."

"Why?"

"I don't know."

Jess groaned. "So we're back to mirrors, I guess? Maybe finding the mirror that was in the room with her when she died? I feel like we've made no progress whatsoever."

"We haven't," I said flatly.

Mary wrenched her head around on her shoulders. There was an unsettling crunch, like her vertebrae had popped back into alignment. She shoved at the ground to dislodge her body from the packed dirt but couldn't quite manage it. I knew better than to hope that she was down for good.

I grabbed Jess's sleeve and ran toward the second building. "We have to get Kitty and Dell." I hesitated outside of the front door, the thick, black smoke pouring out and swallowing all the good air.

Behind me, Mary groaned.

"I'll stay down here in case she gets up again. Get Dell and Kitty." Jess whirled on the ghost, the salt boxes poised and ready to fire.

I jerked my T-shirt over my nose and barreled ahead. My eyes ached the moment I stepped into the house. The fire still burned, and it was hotter than Hell inside. I fumbled for the railing of the stairs only to find no railing. Through the smoke, I could faintly see its shape in the middle of the living room.

Mary snapped the railing off in her rage.

I hugged the wall and climbed toward the balcony. I plowed my way toward the door leading to the roof. Opening it blasted me with more smoke and I took another deep breath from under the T-shirt.

Onward I pressed, feeling faint and sick and sore. The hatch door had been splintered apart under Mary's brute force. I climbed up and into the cupola. The couch was pushed against the opposite wall. The fire licked higher, reaching toward the crow's face in the stained glass window.

I was half-blind as I bumbled my way toward the widow's walk. I could make out Dell's shape near the chimney. She'd collapsed, her mouth gaping open, a pool of blood beneath her cheek. I rushed to her, my hand sweeping over her sweaty forehead and down to her neck in search of a pulse. I didn't feel anything, but when I shifted my fingers, life thrummed against my pads.

"Kitty! Are you here?" I called out.

"Oh, my God. You're okay. I've been trying to get up the roof, but I keep sliding back. I saw her fall. Is she dead?" Kitty was still on the side of the roof I'd leapt from. I looped my arms under Dell's and pulled her toward the break in the railing, grunting with exertion.

"Mary's out front, but Jess is holding her off. Our best bet is to get Dell down from back here if we can. We have to run."

The farther away from the cupola I got, the better I could see. Kitty was halfway up the roof side, the sledgehammer abandoned behind her. Her brown hair was matted to her scalp with sweat. Her green eyes were huge. She was rosy all over, her fear flushing her from head to toe.

"I'm so glad to see you," she said, stretching up as I bent down. Between the two of us, we were able to slide Dell down the decline. Dell moaned as she hit a bump, but otherwise went unharmed.

"Hey! Is she okay?" Jess jogged around the conservatory side, her bruised face tilted up at us with concern.

"She's passed out, but she's alive!" Kitty called. "Do you think you can catch her?"

"Yes." Jess dropped the salt boxes and reached up her arms toward the roof overhang. Kitty lay flat on her stomach across the roof, using her own weight as an anchor. Getting a grip on Dell was tricky, but she figured out that she could hold on to her feet better than her hands when she lowered her down. "Where's Mary?" I shouted.

Jess jumped up to grab Dell's hands, reeling her aunt in as much as she could before Kitty dropped her. "I salted her. It's fine."

Kitty counted three, two, one and eased Dell down. I watched her body slip past the ledge and from my sight. I glanced back at the smoking cupola. I felt like a scared failure. We'd dedicated the last month to putting Bloody Mary Worth away. Some of us died for it. Solving her murder should have ended everything. Destroying her remains worked in all the movies and TV shows. But it was a lie. Nothing had changed. We were back to hunches, conjecture, and mirrors.

"Jump down. I'll catch you," I heard Jess say to Kitty. Below, Dell sprawled across the dry grass, her head tilted back, her mouth hanging open. Blood drizzled from the corners of her lips. Jess stood beside her, arms lifted up again in wait. Kitty looked back at me from the roof, her hand outstretched.

"Come on. We'll get out of here."

She probably meant Hawthorne House, but I was ready to exit the situation for good.

Enough. I'm sorry, Anna. Cody.

I was about to slide down the roof toward Kitty when the blur of motion zoomed around the corner. There was no time to react. There was no time to *run*. Jess stood on the ground, awaiting us, and then she didn't. She flew back, pinned beneath a snarling, blood-crazed Mary. She was a broken, disjointed collection of smoking parts, her body crushed and mangled, but that didn't stop her. Her gray, rotten arm lifted above her head before she thrust it down at Jess's neck. Her claws dug into the sides of Jess's throat, fingernails piercing the soft, supple skin before she wrenched her hand away.

Pink, ragged flesh sundered from its proper place.

The screams were Kitty's, not Jess's, because Jess didn't have time to scream. She gurgled wetly, red painting her chest, the ghost above her, the ground to either side of her. Her hand clutched the wound, blood surging from between her fingers with the panicked beats of her heart. Her legs and arms jolted, her body convulsed.

Seconds later, she went still.

Kitty wheezed, her asthma strangling the air from her lungs. I did nothing. I couldn't think. I couldn't act. Jess was dead. All the things I'd said to her—all the accusations. The distance between us that hadn't been there for ten years.

But I couldn't forgive. Not in time.

Jess didn't deserve the ending she got.

No one did.

"No," I whispered, shaking my head. "Jess? JESS!"

There was no answer.

Behind me, the cupola crackled. One of the regular windows had split under the pressure of the heat, fire surging up to lick at the walls. Trembling, I peered at the spiderweb crack in the glass. I looked down at Mary.

Perhaps it was the trauma of what I'd just witnessed that

made my brain twitch. Perhaps it was Mary standing over Jess and covered in her blood, her head tilting back as she watched Kitty. But as I stood there on the widow's walk, a puzzle piece rotated inside my head. I'd thought burning the bones would complete the Mary Worth picture, but it discounted something very important. Something Jess had said not two minutes ago.

So we're back to looking for mirrors.

No, we weren't. We were back to looking for *shine*—anything that shined could have trapped Mary's soul to this plane. She was in all reflective surfaces. Elsa had put the toy on my head because she was trying to tell me to look up at the bird. At the Hawthorne bird.

The Hawthorne bird made of glass.

When they'd opened up that trunk to throw Philip in with Mary, she'd cleaved to the stained glass. To the crow.

"The sledgehammer," I said to Kitty just as Mary lunged up at the roof's edge. Her fingers latched for a moment before she dropped back down again. Mary leapt a second time, getting a grip, but falling with a snarl. I could hear her harsh, dry laughter from the ground as Kitty scrambled up the slope. Mary lunged and lunged, intent on scaling the roof.

"Kitty, the sledgehammer," I repeated, my voice as calm as I could manage.

Kitty stared at me, tears running rivers over her face. I motioned at the sledgehammer. She extended it my way, yelping when Mary clung to the edge of the roof and managed to pull up her torso. She dangled from the side and growled, her mouth gaping open, her new teeth gleaming. She heaved herself up with another trill of raspy laughter. Kitty withdrew as far as she could, the angle of the roof limiting her escape path.

I ran into the cupola. It was smoky and black and awful, but I didn't hesitate. I pulled back the sledgehammer and aimed it at the stained glass bird. It cracked but didn't give. Mary screeched from outside. I did it again, bringing the hammer around with as much fury as I could muster. The metal head crashed through the Hawthorne crest, splintering the surface, shattering the crow and raining sparkling glass.

I backed from the cupola and toward the widow's walk. Mary was only feet away from Kitty, but instead of pressing her advantage, she froze, her eyes wide. She looked past us to the broken glass on the ground. There was a small whine and then she skulked away like a wounded animal.

Her foot fell off first. Then her fingers, followed by a leg. As each piece disconnected from the whole, it disintegrated to dust, floating away in the writhing smoke clouds. Mary whimpered, staring at me with her shriveled black eye and her milky stolen one before they plummeted from her skull and turned to ash.

Mary Worth crumbled to bits before us, the glass that bound her to this world shattered.

∞

Somewhere to the south, sirens wailed. I slid down the roof to join Kitty on the eave, gathering her up and guiding her toward the conservatory. I made the first jump, no longer afraid, like all fear had been tapped from my body. I helped Kitty down, then I sat beside the still-warm body of Jess McAllister and her struggling aunt, my sneaker resting in the growing pool of blood.

Brownies and Girl Scouts and family vacations. Summers by the lake with campfires and canoes. Stories of first kisses. Secrets told. Late-night texts. Fights and make-ups and everything in between. We were a team, Jess and I.

Now she's Mary Worth's last victim.

The sobs took me by surprise. They made my chest and stomach ache. Kitty wrapped her arms around my shoulders, and I pulled her close, watching the smoke rising from the roof of Hawthorne House through a blur of tears.

Kitty pressed her dry lips to my cheek as the ambulance pulled up the drive.

∞

The aftermath was a whirlwind. The EMTs tried to resuscitate Jess in the ambulance to no avail. Dell was admitted to the hospital and stabilized despite her blood loss. The sheriff was able to save most of the second house. I later learned he had it bulldozed anyway.

We had no reason to stay in Solomon's Folly after Mary's fall. The ghoul was gone, or as gone as we could make her. The only reason we lingered on Hawthorne property at all was so Kitty could ask the sheriff what we should tell our parents about Jess.

Sheriff Hawthorne eyed us from under the brim of his navy blue hat, the corners of his mouth hidden by his heavy mustache.

"There was an accident. Jessica fell from the roof."

No, she didn't. She had her throat ripped out.

It wasn't supposed to end like this.

We climbed into the car and pulled away from Hawthorne House for what I hoped would be the last time. Lydia Hawthorne stood on the front porch with her brother, Bran, watching our retreat. She lifted a hand in a wave, but I didn't reciprocate. I couldn't. I was too shaken.

So was Kitty. She didn't talk for a full half hour. The only sounds she could make were quiet snivels. They echoed my whimpers.

I want my mother. I want to go home.

I rested my head against the window and closed my eyes. Weary. Afraid. Sad.

Winning had never felt so much like losing before.

We were on the last leg of the drive when I remembered the letter in my pocket. I pulled it out, examining the thick vellum paper with age discoloration along the edges. It seemed important and yet not at all in the wake of Mary's destruction.

I opened it all the same.

My name is Elizabeth Jane Hawthorne, daughter of Seymour Hawthorne and Margaret Pepper Hawthorne. I was the wife of Philip Starkcrowe III, and then the wife of Aaron Jenson. Like all Hawthornes, I was born and shall die in Solomon's Folly.

This is my confession.

There is nothing special about me. I am not particularly pretty nor am I scholarly like my brother Matthew. I do not have Alexander's wit or sense of humor. My years walking this earth have only proved that I am a bad wife and a terrible daughter. My marriages failed with no love or children to show for my time. My father speaks of our legacy like it is a reason to rise in the morning. Solomon's Folly is our pride. It is sad then that his lone daughter is as wicked as Solomon himself. I swore four years ago that I would never again come to this box of regret, which is what these remains represent, but I feel I cannot go to the good rest without confessing my sins. No pastor wishes to listen to what would be construed as mad prattling, and when I try to speak with my father, he pretends that he cannot hear me. This secret is my burden.

My dislike of Mary Worth started through no fault of hers. I was and am foolish when it comes to my affections, and I have loved Thomas Adderly for as long as I've known the meaning of the word. He is tall and handsome and has good teeth. They are very white and straight.

As a girl, I would have done anything for him to smile upon me, and truth be told, I suspected one day he would. I am a Hawthorne, and Hawthornes always get what they think they want. I presumed Thomas's affections were a matter of time. But patience is a virtue and I am not virtuous enough. When I discovered that Thomas hung his hat upon the Worth girl, I grew incensed. The Worths were poor. Comely, yes, and the mother seemed kind, but they didn't deserve what I deserved. I was only thirteen and stupid.

Mary stood between me and the man of my heart, so I did what any petulant girl would do: I tortured Mary. For years I afflicted her with hurtful words and petty revenges that she never warranted. I should have tired of it quickly, but the cruelties entertained my friends. Their laughter made me brave.

I remember the first day Philip Starkcrowe preached at Southbridge Parish, after Pastor Renault's relocation to the Berkshires. I had no idea Philip would be my one-day husband, but then, our sin eventually brought us together in unholy matrimony. That day, I stood with my family after Sunday service watching Philip's reaction to Hannah Worth. She was the fairest of us all, too beautiful for Solomon's Folly, and despite being five years her junior, Philip could not hide his fascination. When I noticed, Mary noticed, too. She called attention to it in her own quiet way, and he instantly loathed her for throttling his ardor.

I will never say much good about Philip, but I cannot deny his craftiness. He wished to pursue the Worth matriarch, and having a bold daughter provided an opportunity to spend time with the family. He had no interest in Mary's betterment, but he claimed otherwise, and Mrs. Worth reacted as any mother scared for her child would. She trusted that a man of God would never abuse the privileges of his station and let him tutor Mary.

Hannah was naïve.

I saw Philip's disdain as validation of my own crusade. Sarah, Meredith, Agnes, and I would go to the church after lessons under the guise of spirituality, but it was to see what awful thing befell Mary that day and delight in it. At times, Philip would tie Mary's left arm behind her back and a ruler to her spine while she copied Bible text. Other times, she would be forced to scrub the vestibule with a small brush only for Philip to stomp through with muddied boots so she'd have to begin anew. He struck her often. He threatened to have her immured with the lunatics. He locked her in the basement of the church for hours at a time.

How he thought tormenting the daughter would endear him to the mother, I do not know. Perhaps he assumed Hannah would believe his word over Mary's. In the end it did not matter. Hannah drowned. Philip never spoke of her after our marriage, and I never asked, because the truth scared me. Everyone knew that woman did not jump to her death. She went walking one night and never came home. We all had our suspicions, but the constable did not wish to call a godly man a liar. Perhaps that was fear for his soul. Perhaps it was lack of evidence beyond a body in the reeds of the river. Thus, a murderer walked free. I will not deny that I laughed at Mary's misfortune. To claim otherwise is a lie, and I refuse to perpetuate any more of those while I still have breath to breathe.

I thought Mary would relocate to Boston with her sister, but

Mary was given into the care of the very man who orphaned her. It made little sense. Even my father, who rarely involved himself in lesser matters, commented that the girl belonged elsewhere, but no one made a fuss. Constance might have insisted upon her removal, but she had just welcomed a baby son.

October 28, 1864, was when my life changed for the worse. The day began like any other: breakfast with my brothers, lessons, lunch at my father's office, and gathering at the church with Sarah, Meredith, and Agnes when we grew bored with needlepoint. While Philip was horrid to Mary, he seemed to relish our company. Agnes quite fancied herself in love with him. He didn't return the affection. Agnes was given the courtesy afforded the Hawthornes and those they held dear.

Mary was locked in the basement upon our arrival. We'd seen the pastor strike her across the mouth the previous day, bloodying her before thrusting her into the dark. Sarah had come up with the moniker of Bloody Mary, and we whispered it to her through the door like idiotic children. Something was changed that day, though. Mary was formidable like never before. Philip was in a red-faced frenzy. Mary threw herself against the door hard enough that it rattled on the hinges, demanding that he release her.

"You can rot in there for all I care, you treacherous harlot," Philip snarled, not realizing that we four stood behind the pews.

Mary slammed harder upon the door.

I felt unsettled by this exchange, and Agnes fared no better. She pulled upon my sleeve, pleading for us to go. Would that I could rewind the time, but curiosity got the better of me and

I thrust her away. She left with Meredith at her side. Sarah remained with me out of loyalty, clasping my hand and watching the pastor pace the church like a caged lion.

He sensed our presence then, whirling on us with a look of fury. I feared he would deliver his vengeful wrath upon us, but he exited the church instead, I assumed for a walk to placate his ire.

"You will let me out this instant. If you wish to act the lech, find yourself a doxy, Pastor!"

Mary could not have manufactured the claim for our benefit—she did not even know we were there. Philip had tried to compromise her and she rebelled against his advances. It was more proof that he was not the courtly gentleman Agnes fancied.

For the first time, I felt pity for Mary Worth. I had not quite yet come to the conclusion that I had wronged her, but I was on the path to understanding. I approached the door. Sarah tried to stop me, whispering that I could not act against the pastor, but I did not see it as defiance. I'm a Hawthorne. The only people Hawthornes must abide are the elders in their own House.

"Mary?" I called through the door.

There were more furious kicks on the other side. "Leave me, Elizabeth. I want nothing to do with you or your broody hens."

"Hush and I'll let you out." Only I had taunted her thusly not two days ago. She could not have known I had changed my song. When she pummeled the door, I hesitated, but my convictions spurred me onward and I fussed with the lock. The pastor returned at the wrong time. Seeing me at the door, he shouted for me to stop, but I did not know he approached. I did not know he was still consumed with fury. All I knew was that the door was swinging open. Mary stood in her white frock, astounded that I'd been kind. She was so very thin that the dress hung loose upon her body. It was smeared in dirt, and there were bugs on it from her tenure in the basement.

What happened next is hard for me to relay. The pastor shoved past Sarah to wrench the door from my grasp. We scrambled as he tried to close it, and I held it open with my inferior strength. Mary shouted and barged forward, surely afraid that Philip would send her back into the recesses of the church.

He pushed her.

He would call it an accident, but I saw his expression when he turned on her. None of his anger had abated when he put his hand over her face, nestled it into his palm, and shoved. The stairs were slippery. Her head struck a step and cracked open, spilling her blood across the stone. She sprawled on the floor like a broken doll.

This is not where I became an accessory to Philip's crime. That occurred when he convinced two hysterical girls that we would be punished for Mary's death if we did not follow his lead. He pulled us into the basement with him, Sarah holding the lantern as he frantically dug into the floor with a shovel. He didn't go deep; far enough that he could lay the bricks flat after Mary's burial. I watched him haul her limp body into that pit. I watched him shovel wet mud on her dress from the feet up.

I watched her eyes blink open as he covered her head.

I never told him she was alive. I don't know that it would have mattered. He likely would have finished what he started. I will not make excuses for my actions. It was an evil deed committed by a scared, stupid, selfish girl. I was so afraid my father would discover my transgression, I let Mary Worth be buried alive. With Mary interred, Philip told us we must pray for forgiveness from God, and that we must never speak of what happened. I did as instructed because I worried the pastor would put the blame on me and my friends—that my public disdain of the Worth girl would incriminate me. That a frail woman's word would never matter more than that of the man charged with our immortal souls. Philip used that fear to control us.

I barely slept at night, and Sarah was prone to fits of weeping, but we maintained our silence. Meanwhile, the pastor convinced everyone that Mary escaped his care to be with her sister in Boston. He played the bereaved guardian ever hopeful for his ward's safety.

These were the first of the lies but by no means the last. Joseph Simpson arrived in town a week later. He is Constance Worth's husband and a sophisticated lawyer from the city. His black hair and blue eyes would have set the girls to tittering had he come at any other time, but considering his business with The Folly, he was met with suspicion and disdain. It did not deter him. He had many questions, and he came armed with accusations. He knew of Mary's trials with the pastor. He also knew of my history, though he filtered his inquiries through my father.

Hours after Mr. Simpson's appearance, Philip shadowed my father's doorstep. I was at lessons at the time, but when I came home, both of them awaited me in the front study. My father reserved this room for work, but I was called before the judge's desk not as his daughter but as a potential murderess. It was the first time my father ever struck me. I had always been his sweet girl, but from that moment on he treated me as a stranger. Philip had poisoned his mind about the events in the church. It had been my hand that shoved Mary. It had been my impassioned moment that led to her demise. In his iteration, he struggled to preserve Mary's life against me. Philip painted himself my savior, the man who valiantly buried the body in the church's basement to protect my reputation and the Hawthorne name.

I don't know what my father believed, but the threat of scandal spurred him to action. Mary's body was to be moved to a less obvious location—likely the swamp, where her mother rested. Also, I would marry Philip Starkcrowe in two weeks' time. It was, as my father so coldly put it, insurance. Philip would be part of the family and thus beholden to the Hawthorne name. Our unborn children were ties that would permanently bind.

I protested, but it did no good. Asserting that Philip was responsible not for one but two Worth deaths changed little. "It's too late, Elizabeth. Had you been a victim of circumstance, you would have come to me a week ago. The innocent have nothing to hide and so they do not bother trying." At dinner that night, word reached us that Joseph Simpson had procured a proper warrant to launch an investigation. It would inevitably land him on my doorstep—my mistreatment of Mary was not unknown. Though the constable was one of my father's closest friends, there were some legalities neither of them could circumvent, which is how I ended up in the church basement after dark with my brothers digging up Mary Worth's corpse. Father insisted I go, any delicacies granted me by my womanhood no longer a consideration.

Simpson questioned Philip at the jail that night, which granted me and my brothers a slice of time to conduct our illicit deed. I remember the revolting smell and the gray tinge to Mary's skin. I remember a piece of her body breaking away and Alexander hastily shoving it into his burlap sack. Matthew replaced the stones of the floor while Alexander and I dragged Mary to the cart. No one dared to enter the swamp at night, so Mary was brought back to Hawthorne House.

I feared discovery, but Alexander assured me that Father had it well in hand. There was a trunk. They tried shoving the sack inside but Mary did not fit, and so they made her fit. I will not go into details. Into the cupola she went. I did not find it a terribly good hiding spot, but then our house man, the Greek Leopold, came into play. I was told to bathe, my clothes taken and burned along with my brothers'. By the time I dressed in my nightclothes, Leopold was at work in the attic. By morning, a pair of chairs, a bookshelf, a portrait of my grandfather, and gas lanterns affixed the wall that had not been there twelve hours before. Mary rested beneath the stained glass window, hidden from the world by a lovely retreat.

Simpson's investigations continued for some time, long past my marriage to Philip, but he returned to his wife in January of 1865 with no answers about the missing Mary. By then, I had taken up residence in the eastern half of Hawthorne House with my husband. The gossipmongers quieted for the most part.

In the earliest parts of our marriage, Philip was courteous. We acted the parts of any newly married couple, feigning a joy we did not feel. My guilt weighed heavily at first, but over time, it grew easier to live with myself. I tried to forget Mary Worth and concentrate on pleasing my new husband. While Philip was stern and demanded near constant veneration to our God, he was easily pleased with his favorite stew and ample time to himself.

Our trouble began when he grew restless. As I stated before, I am not as lovely as other girls. I am plain with milquetoast skin and drab brown hair. My nose is too long, my eyes as dark as pitch. While I cannot say for certain that Philip had walked Eden's garden enough to know the many paths, his dealings with the Worth women gave me reason to believe it so.

After two months, the violence began. It was always below the neck so my dresses would hide the bruises. My Hawthorne pride would not allow me to broach this subject with my father. He barely spoke to me anymore, our familial bond tainted beyond repair. Begging him to intervene was impossible.

It was six months into the marriage, four beneath Philip's punishing blows, when the situation became untenable. I made his stew, but he complained through every bite. When he threw the food into the fire and told me it wasn't fit for a dog, I left the table and climbed the stairs. My intent was to go to sleep. He misconstrued it as rebellion.

He chased me up the stairs and grabbed my hair, striking me across the mouth until I tasted blood. The things he screamed were hard to parse. Scripture and profanity blended seamlessly. The punch to my eye almost blinded me, but it was the shaking that scared me most. I felt my feet slipping on the landing, and instinct took over. I did not intend to shove him, but that is what happened. I must have caught him off guard as he fell backward, immediately striking his head upon one of the wooden steps.

Not unlike Mary Worth, Philip Starkcrowe died upon the stairs, his neck snapped, head lolling to the side at a wrong angle.

I did not make the same mistake twice. I informed my father immediately. While he was not pleased, he did not berate me, for which I can thank my blackened, swollen eye. The story he concocted was that Philip, dissatisfied with his plain wife, abandoned the town to seek his fortunes elsewhere. Railway tickets were purchased in his name. His bags were packed and promptly disappeared, no doubt in the swamp somewhere. I asked what we would do with Philip's body. Father cast me a withering look and again called upon Leopold.

I was not a superstitious girl. While Agnes and Meredith conducted séances to speak with the other side, grimoires ever at the ready, I did not subscribe to such nonsense. However, even I could see the folly in putting the remains of the murderer in with the victim. It tempted fate. I protested as much, but I was promptly dismissed as the wall was taken down. Philip was dumped into the trunk atop Mary Worth. The wall closed them in together.

Opening that trunk was the worst thing they could have done. She anchored herself to this world and began her quest for vengeance.

She appeared in the glass of my mirror as I went to bed, peering out at me as if she existed on the other side of a door. I thought I would expire from fear. She was a hideous thing. The flesh on her bones sagged, a thin growth of mold covering her face and her one remaining ear. Her jaw looked loose, as if it would fall off her face if she turned her head too fast. One of her arms was cut off at the elbow. I correlated it to a cut Alexander had made to get her into the trunk all those months ago.

I ran from my room, screaming that Mary Worth had come to get me. I was alone in the eastern wing, and so I ran to the western, across the yard to my father's house. He was out, likely ensuring that the truth about Philip's death did not leak or cause trouble. My mother did what she could to calm me, eventually dosing my tea with laudanum to put me to sleep. For the first time in fifteen years, I slept upon her breast, my arms wrapped around her.

I spent all the next day convincing myself that the vision of Mary was a reaction to trauma. All of that shattered when a weepy Agnes arrived on my doorstep, claiming to have seen the ghost. My fear returned twofold. Not only had Mary appeared the very night Philip was put to rest beside her, but to one of my friends? It seemed improbable, but then both Meredith and Sarah showed up, equally frightened. They'd seen Mary, too.

This presented a set of challenges for me. Firstly, I was supposed to be grieving Philip's betrayal, not frantic about a girl who died six months previous. Secondly, my father would never listen if I told him that he had to take down the wall and separate their bodies. I did not know what to do.

The decision was made for me when the constable arrived, asking after Philip. The brevity of the questioning told me that my father had already taken care of the mess. I did not pretend to be upset. With my pulpy face, it was unnecessary. I could shed no tears for a man so wicked.

The girls stayed with me that night, all of us dreading another encounter with the phantom. Mary never came. When the next day passed and she did not come, I was relieved. Perhaps Mary had expressed her discontent with her entombment and had moved on to the better afterlife she deserved.

On April 30, 1865, Sarah Ashby went missing. Her sister reported that Sarah went into her dressing room and never came out again. I did not blame it upon the ghost, for it did not occur to me that such a thing could be possible. Oh, how I mourned my dear friend. Sarah had been as a sister to me. I felt her loss so keenly, it was as if a part of me had gone with her.

The town rallied around me, abandoned by my husband, now missing my nearest and dearest friend, but it did little for my heavy heart. No trace was ever found of Sarah, nor was any trace found of Meredith when she disappeared on June 19, 1865, or Agnes when she disappeared on August 4, 1865.

The public outcry was swift. They assumed there was a murderer in our midst. Watch groups formed, the men taking up weapons and going on patrols, but no evidence was ever found. The initiative fizzled quickly, but when the only common thread among the disappearances was that each of the girls went into a room alone and never came back, what could they expect? My father had the audacity to call me to his office and ask me bluntly if I had anything to do with their deaths. The poison dripped from my tongue when I told him that, no, my murderous ways were reserved for the abusive men he married me to.

His response to that was to tell me that I would be married again by year's end to a man by the name of Aaron Jenson, and he would appreciate it kindly if I did not strike him down, as the trunk was out of space.

I was too despondent to argue. I had, by then, lost everyone dear to me. My friends were dead. My brothers were disgusted by me, thinking me a fallen woman. My father treated me like a shadow. My mother was kind sometimes, but only when my father was elsewhere. A second husband was nothing compared with these things. I deemed Aaron an ignorable nuisance before ever meeting him.

Father informed me that I would be attending a dinner party with him and Mother to meet with Mr. Jenson. I was to act the part of the dutiful daughter, smile when I ought to smile, and not eat too much for fear of diminishing my value to a man twice my age.

As I powdered my nose, I looked in the mirror, but instead of seeing my own reflection, I saw Mary's face. It is hard to describe her as improved from the last appearance, but her skin was firmer, the missing arm replaced, and her jaw aligned. She was still quite dead and awful, but somehow more alive.

I shouted and hustled from the room to join my parents. My mother asked if I was well, but my father snapped at me to comport myself with dignity—that I would not shame the Hawthornes yet again by alienating the one man left in Solomon's Folly who would have me. I closed my eyes during the carriage ride, deep breaths helping me quell my fear.

Somehow, Aaron found me enchanting despite my plainness, my dearth of conversation skills, and my avoidance of my own reflection. I found him tedious with his grizzled whiskers, monotone prattling, and mustard-stained vest.

My father had Philip declared dead in October after his luggage was found on the edges of the swamp. Aaron and I were married in November. I saw Mary more frequently after that, sometimes in my vanity, which I had removed from my room, but most often in the panes of glass in the house windows. Aaron thought me a skittish thing, but having a dead girl gazing at you from mirrors would rob even the bravest of their resolve.

I plunged the household into dark with thick drapes and shades. My husband did not seem to mind, but he did not have a passionate disposition and was quite content to sit on the porch swing until the snows came. He was an old man with a young wife, hoping for a passel of children before death caught up to him.

Mary took to haunting other things. Plates, candlesticks, hairbrushes. I purged the household of anything that could house the ghost's visage. I was desperate to relocate Mary's remains from the attic, but I had an ignorant husband always in attendance, my father lived on the other side of the estate and would never allow it, and I hadn't the faintest idea of how to get through the wall on my own. My one attempt with a hammer resulted in a tiny hole, through which, dear letter, you shall be thrust upon completion.

I am quite near completion.

I cannot run from Mary much longer, nor do I believe I warrant the escape. There is little one can do without light, and I lack it so often that I have long swaths of time to ponder my life's choices. I see now that the specter is my punishment for years of unkindness. It is my comeuppance for watching Philip bury Mary beneath the mud and stone. Seeing her in the glass, I understand how my friends disappeared. She took them. Whether that was to punish them for their transgressions or to punish me for mine, I do not know. The latter hurts my heart, but it is no less than I deserve.

While I can live without windows and sterling, I cannot live without water, which is where I see Mary most lately. I drink it in the dark so there is no reflection. I bathe in the dark as well. My options run thin, and I find instead of being fearful, I am weary.

Sorry and weary. This is no way to live. All hail the great and mighty Hawthornes, a house built upon the bones of those we wronged.

E.H.

Acknowledgments

I wrote this book twice.

The first time, I was in no condition to *exist*, never mind put words to paper. My mother was diagnosed with cancer in January 2014, in the early stages of this book's development. I had deadlines, and I trucked on despite the strain—despite Mom's chemo and my constant worry that I was going to lose someone so special. The end result wasn't pretty. I wrote a book that was a product of my headspace. It didn't satisfy me, nor would it have satisfied any reader who set eyes upon it. I wouldn't show it to my oh-so-patient editor, Tracey Keevan. I wouldn't even show it to my agent, Miriam Kriss, who's seen all of my word atrocities for the past five years. It was that rough.

Fast-forward eight months. Mom persevered and is, as of this writing, doing remarkably well. She's always been excellent at sassing the world at large, and thanks to an incredible team of doctors at Brigham and Women's, will continue to do so for years to come.

We were lucky. It was over for us. With that weight off my shoulders, I was able to sit down and write *Mary: Unleashed* a second time, the way it deserved to be written. I couldn't have done that without the support of my family, friends, and publishing circle. I'm so grateful to have my mother here. I'm so grateful that people helped me, so I could help her. It's funny how kindness trickles down like that, bestowed upon one person so they can share it with another—and believe me, there was an abundance of kindness. More than I can possibly call attention to in a short acknowledgments page.

So, to everyone who spared a prayer, who offered an ear, a hug, and encouragement when the fog was thickest, thank you. This book wouldn't be possible without you.